# PRETENDERS LIKE US

MARY CAMPISI

MARY CAMPISI BOOKS, LLC

# DESCRIPTION

Ethan Nance lives his life guided by analyses and spreadsheets and avoids anything resembling an emotion. He made that mistake once and suffered the disastrous consequences of opening his heart. Ethan's a firm believer that data collection, objectivity, and deductive reasoning are the keys to eliminating surprises and reducing disappointment.

*And then he meets Vanessa Rodelle,* a woman who challenges, confuses, and disturbs him in a way no woman ever has.

Vanessa Rodelle once believed in happily-ever-after, but reality taught her the hard lesson of following her heart. It's much safer to let data and facts guide her.

*And then she meets Ethan Nance,* a man she can't analyze, understand, or ignore.

Ethan and Vanessa might not believe in destiny, but one hot steamy night together changes everything, and no spreadsheets or logic can explain or erase it. Can they learn to trust and open their hearts once again for a chance at real love? It's going to get very interesting and the residents of the small town of Reunion Gap will offer their stories, guidance, and support to help this meant-to-be couple find their happily-ever-after. The only question left is will Ethan and Vanessa take the risk and listen to their hearts?

**Reunion Gap series:**

Book One: *Strangers Like Us*

Book Two: *Liars Like Us*

Book Three: *Lovers Like Us*

Book Four: *Couples Like Us*

Book Five: *Guilty Like Us*

Book Six: *Pretenders Like Us*

*I would like to dedicate this book in memory of my reader friend, Betty Weiner. Betty wrote me a letter years ago when she read one of my books. She sent the letter to my publisher who rerouted it to me. This was at a time before the digital and social media world exploded so the ease of correspondence between readers and writers was a bit of a challenge. Betty and I began exchanging Christmas cards, well wishes, and updates on our lives and I truly looked forward to hearing from her. I lost track of her a few years ago and was saddened when her daughter reached out to inform me of her passing. I think Betty would have enjoyed Pretenders Like Us, and I would like to honor her with this dedication.*

# 1

E than Nance avoided small towns, emotion, and women he might actually be interested in. He had his reasons but he'd buried them years ago, and that's exactly where they stayed...until his best friend announced he was tying the knot in the place where he grew up. Reunion Gap was a small town in the foothills of the Allegheny mountains that boasted family, community, and good-old fashioned hospitality. Just what Ethan didn't need—more busybodies asking too many questions that were none of their concern. He'd heard it all before, and this town was no different.

*You sure are handsome and look at that suit!*

*Do you have a girlfriend?*

*No?*

*Oh.* And then *Why not?*

*I'll bet we could introduce you to a few 'potentials'.*

A side eye, a smile. *But you don't seem like the type to need help with that sort of thing.*

*No indeed.*

No, he did not need help because he wasn't looking for a date, a girlfriend, and certainly not a wife. Why did people think a plus-one was mandatory to attend a wedding? Or to navigate life? Or to suck in a full breath? The whole idea of a "significant other" sounded painful and unnecessary. And for the sake of objectivity, say he invited someone to this event, what then? Would she understand it was a one-time only offer and not an invitation to share anything else—not his life, his bed, or his name?

Probably not because this was a wedding, an out-of-town one that involved Ethan as the best man. A "date" would make assumptions and it wouldn't matter how many times or with how much conviction he insisted otherwise, she would believe her presence meant something to him...meant something *about* them...except there was no *them*. Never would be. Why couldn't they understand that he wasn't the type to sugarcoat or spin a tale where a woman was concerned? None of that because what was the point? He was a straight-up, tell-it-like-it-is kind of guy who didn't have the energy or the time for tears, misunderstandings, or broken furniture.

If Daniel weren't his best friend and Ethan hadn't agreed to the best man gig, he wouldn't be on the verge of breaking the vow he made twelve years ago. *I'll never attend another wedding. No thanks. Never again.*

But he was going to break that vow because Daniel and Meredith deserved it. Still, it didn't mean he planned to change his stance on weddings or his belief that they were overdone confections smothered in promises and forevers with low percentages of making it past the five-year mark. Daniel and Meredith might be the exception. It was obvious the two loved each other, and if a nonbeliever like Ethan could see it, then didn't he owe it to them to show up and smile as though he believed in happily-ever-after?

Yes, he did and he would not disappoint.

He drove to Reunion Gap late one afternoon, prepared to

suffer through a few days of too many questions, too much emotion, and way too many carbs. What he'd found surprised him. Yes, there were a few casual inquiries and tsunamis of emotion and no doubt carbs ruled. But the people didn't poke around for answers or make assumptions about him. Meredith's brother, Tate, was a standup guy with a solid business sense and an eye for style that made conversations with him almost worth the extra emotion *and* the carbs.

Then there was Vanessa Rodelle, Meredith's business partner, the woman he *could* be interested in if life and circumstances were different. Beautiful, classy, intelligent. He'd been curious about her since the first time he'd typed her name in an online search as part of an information-gathering project Daniel had given him. The "project" was Meredith Alexander. Yeah, that had been a real mess but at least Daniel and Meredith had gotten past that, hence the upcoming nuptials.

And Vanessa Rodelle? The data he'd found proved intriguing; the degrees, the accomplishments, the honors and awards. She'd been on the board of five different committees in the past two years! Did the woman ever rest? What did she do for fun? Did she have fun or was she a working machine? No idea, but he'd been determined to find out.

Maybe he should have asked himself why he cared, but he didn't. Nope, he just catalogued Vanessa Rodelle as a puzzle he wanted to solve. They'd talked on the phone a few times about their roles as coordinators and keepers of schedules for Daniel and Meredith's upcoming wedding. Who would have thought he'd turn into a quasi-wedding planner? It wasn't horrible, as long as he could focus on dates, time, and numbers, all of which he compiled into a formula-driven spreadsheet. Vanessa loved the spreadsheets, added a few formulas of her own. Very impressive. Of course, there were considerations in regard to color, fabric, and floral choices, and who better than Tate Alexander to take over that task? The business of wedding planning wasn't so bad when you could delegate to qualified individuals.

The other benefit of "assisting" with wedding activities was Ethan's phone time with Vanessa. He'd been curious enough about the woman to suggest they meet for a drink to brainstorm wedding details, but she'd declined. *Too busy, but thanks for the offer.* Hmm. A comment like that could mean anything. Maybe she *was* too busy or maybe she just wasn't interested—in the brainstorming *or* him. He'd been half tempted to tell her the offer was for a discussion and a drink, not a long-term relationship. But he'd remained quiet because his gut said this woman was a complicated puzzle and until he figured her out, he should hold back and collect data.

The data collection was key. The other critical skill set was analyzing and remaining objective. If a person kept those traits in mind, he could dissect anything: a situation, a spreadsheet, or an individual. Ethan had become quite adept at the latter and that's why he had no doubt he would solve the curious yet challenging dynamics involving Vanessa Rodelle.

How difficult could it be?

The answer with all of its various complexities hit him square in the chest a few days before the wedding—in Reunion Gap—on the night he finally met her in person. Tate and Charlotte Alexander were hosting a small pre-wedding gathering and of course, Ethan and Vanessa had been invited. The second he spotted Vanessa, he had to suck in several deep breaths. Creative visualization techniques came next. Cloudless skies, gentle streams, snow-capped mountains. One more breath, one last vision of the sky and he was ready.

She stood at the far side of the room: stunning, untouchable, mesmerizing. Like the orchids he tended that detested being fussed over, preferring instead to be left alone.

Ethan assessed and catalogued the woman's looks and style.

Tall, fair-skinned, blonde hair parted on the side accented with a rectangular barrette. He took in the elegant sleekness of the mid-neck-length cut. Did she employ the aid of products and a straightener to achieve the look? And what of the random streaks woven into the blonde? Were they natural or salon acquired? The answer mattered because it revealed a lot about her personality. Wash-and-go with minimal work and no salon color said she could care less what others thought of her looks or her style. However, products, a hair straightener, and an upscale stylist indicated it mattered what others saw *and* what they thought.

Ethan should know. He'd spent years perfecting a look that would convey confidence, style, money, and class. It had been a process, one that became part of him, gave him the ability to detect the small details in others that were at odds with their persona. When he noticed the inconsistencies, he dug deeper, poked around for answers, like the truth.

He zeroed in on Vanessa's face: the cleft chin, the straight nose, the high cheekbones...inched to the eyes. They'd appeared hazel in the online photos, but he wanted a closer look to determine if the online images proved accurate or missed tiny details, like gold or gray flecks. The photos hadn't done justice to her mouth...full red lips...

Curiosity forced Ethan closer to the woman who'd created too many hours of speculation. He would like to say she was just another distraction, like all the others—a way to fill time for a few hours. Or maybe his interest had been an attempt to avoid getting matched up with one of the women who'd been eying him as though he were a party favor. Engaging in conversation with Vanessa would spare him from more offers like the two he'd received a few minutes ago for an after-party "party" and a hot tub visit, no clothing required.

"Vanessa Rodelle, we finally meet."

Those full lips pulled into a slow smile as she extended a hand. "Ethan Nance, the man behind Daniel's success."

"I'm not sure that's true." He took her hand, surprised by the firm grip that could match most men's. "You'll never catch me in a woodshop." A laugh and a shake of his head followed by "Sawdust and a dark suit don't go well together."

"I see." She eased her hand from his, tucked a lock of blonde hair behind her ear. "You might not turn bowls or spend time in a woodshop, but it's quite obvious you're the reason behind Daniel's success."

"It is?" Obvious? Ethan didn't like assumptions and he certainly didn't like his name associated with words like *obvious* when there was nothing obvious about him. But the woman's next words told him her analyzation skills were excellent, possibly as finely honed as his. Not a welcome thought, certainly not a happy one.

"You're more than just the numbers and PR person. You have the ability to spin any situation, *and* you're a fixer."

"That does *not* sound like a compliment." In fact, it bordered on an insult.

A shrug, a hint of a smile. "Consider it an observation." Before he could dispute her words, she tossed out more *observations*. "You studied all of the available information on Meredith and then you devised a plan for Daniel to gain her interest, complete with step-by-step instructions. You even gave him a backstory. Untrue, of course, but believable, especially to a kind heart like Meredith, who wants to save the world. My guess is you figured that out two minutes after you read her file." Pause, a sharp "Yes, I heard about the file."

"I'm sure you did." If she planned to accuse him of manipulating a situation, then she should know the why behind it. "Daniel's my best friend and he needed my help. I'd do it again if he asked me, so if that makes me a manipulator in your eyes, then I guess I am. As for being a fixer? Didn't you help Meredith with her business plan? Convince her to concentrate on one area instead of hopscotching from one idea to another?"

Vanessa cleared her throat, frowned. "I helped her focus. I don't manipulate people or situations."

"Of course, you do, you just call it something else." Oh, she didn't like that and the tiny nostril flare coupled with the way she clenched her wine glass was a giveaway. Too bad. He didn't appreciate words like *fixer* and *manipulator* attached to his name either. Ethan's right temple pinged. *Breathe. Stay calm. Breathe.* Why was he letting her get to him? Nobody could make another person feel a certain way without their permission, right? *Control your thoughts, control your life.* He'd listened to hours of audiobooks, bought scores of hardbacks, and still, he occasionally forgot the message. But he could rework this conversation and where it was headed if he just relaxed and pretended this was a presentation to a client and not an attack on his reputation. A slow breath, a smile, a gentle tone. "Let's call a truce, okay? I've really enjoyed our phone conversations these past several weeks, and I'm sorry I got prickly." A shrug, another smile, and the truth. "People don't usually question me or my motives. Doing the right thing is very important to me, especially where Daniel's concerned."

"I guess I have to acknowledge that while I don't like the fact that you were plotting against Meredith, your motives to help your best friend were honest and decent. I would do the same and if we're being candid, I had my suspicions about Daniel being someone other than who he said he was from the beginning. Meredith tends to rescue strays and people in need and dumps her heart into the cause long before she's vetted it. I don't work that way." More wineglass clenching and a firm "It's dangerous."

"Exactly, right? It's hard to do our job, which is run a business, be a friend, *and* protect the individual from getting hurt when they won't listen. The second I realized Daniel cared about Meredith, I told him to wait until the mess with Harrison Alexander was over before getting involved. But people who believe in destiny and ever-after aren't exactly good listeners."

She laughed, shook her head. "They're the worst with all of that nonsense about love surpassing all. They don't want to hear you tell them the dangers of trusting too soon, too much, too often. They don't want to hear *any* of it, and the more you try to reason with them, the less they share until they aren't sharing anything. Then *boom,* they're in love, it's a disaster, and you're trying to exercise damage control. What a mess."

By disaster, she meant the stories Daniel told Meredith about being a penniless remodeler trying to forge a living with wood-working instead of the truth; he was the man behind the famous bowl-turning company, Langston Turnings. "It's a migraine in the making, no doubt about it."

Her hazel eyes turned bright, the gray flecks in them shifting to silver. "I think they would have eventually gotten past their hurts and reconnected, though it might have taken a while, and there would have been a lot of pain involved. You sidestepped all of that when you sent the video of Daniel unveiling his new work *and* his identity." Her voice dipped, filled with admiration. "Thank you. I'd like to say I'd have done the same, but I'm not sure that's true. What you did says a lot about your character."

How had they gone from accusatory and suspicious to gracious and complimentary? Was she playing him? Trying to get him to relax so she could work an angle? If so, why and what was the angle? The expression and the smile said straight-up serious. He forced himself to relax as he considered the necessity of analyzing her compliments. Ethan always questioned people's motives, considered every possibility so he could be prepared with a plan if one were required. Maybe just this once, he could take someone at her word. Just. This. Once. Besides, he and Vanessa had a common goal now: protect and insulate the soon-to-be newlyweds from distractions, annoyances, and outside interferences like Meredith's father, Harrison Alexander.

"Ethan?"

"Yes?" She had the tiniest dimple in her right cheek when she smiled. And he liked the way—

"You're not used to compliments, are you?" Before he could respond, she added, "You question the sincerity behind the compliment and then you probably examine every word and the emotion attached to it, to determine the basis of the statement."

Was the woman living inside his head? That's exactly what he did! Of course, he wasn't about to straight-out admit that or admit that he often spent hours analyzing the details, so he laughed, because it gave him an extra few seconds to manufacture a semi-intelligent response. "Ah, you've got a background in psychology, don't you?" He shook his head, laughed again. "Interesting commentary. I'm curious, though; is this what *you* do?" The quick intake of breath told him that was *exactly* what she did and her next words told him even more.

"Compliments have a habit of lulling a person into letting down their guard. It makes the person vulnerable. I'm not a fan of them unless they have true merit." She raised a brow. "The one I just gave you does and you can consider yourself worthy because I'm quite stingy with them."

"So, I'm special, is that what you're trying to tell me?" Damn but the woman intrigued him. They shared very similar reasoning skills and thoughts on what did and did not constitute a compliment.

"I didn't say *that*. I merely complimented the behavior."

"Oh, not the person because they're separate." She understood in a few sentences what he'd been trying to explain to Daniel for years.

Her lips twitched. "Exactly."

"Daniel calls me ridiculous."

"Meredith says I have issues."

His shoulders relaxed, and he nodded. "I like to call it being careful. I can't tell you how many times my 'ridiculous' behavior has saved his behind. It's always been my job to protect him—" he paused to give his next words impact "—from all manner of threats, including the ones in short skirts and heels."

Vanessa frowned, didn't try to hide her distaste. "The short skirts and heels better stay away from him or I'll go after them, and I won't be nice about it."

He almost laughed, but the fierce expression said she was dead serious, and something in her tone said she'd do it. "Okay then, looks like we're in agreement on this one. Protect Daniel and Meredith."

"Agreed." She sucked in a breath, lifted her chin. "Some people can't stand to see a happy couple, or they don't under-stand the words *taken* and *not interested.*"

"A wedding ring doesn't stop them either. I'm referring to the one on *their* finger."

"So, married women went after him, too?"

He nodded. "It was nonstop exhausting, and this was when they thought he was just a starving woodworker. Imagine what they might have done if they'd known who he really was?" Just the thought of the chaos that would have created pinched his brain. "Daniel hated it."

"Really? He hated women chasing him?" The raised brow and tone suggested doubt. "He couldn't stand the thought of all those women wanting him?"

Ethan fought the burst of heat slithering up his neck as he recalled the restaurant owner who extended an invitation for drinks, small plates, and big sex at her loft since her husband was out of town. And then there was the brunette who—

"Lots of memories, huh?"

Ethan cleared his throat, snuffed out visions of the women who'd tried to gain access to Daniel. "More headaches than anything else. My job was to protect Daniel, even when he didn't know he needed to be protected."

The slow smile said she liked that answer. A lot. What would she think about the woman who offered Daniel ten thousand a month to be her boy-toy? Before the weekend was over, he might share that story with her. He had a feeling she'd agree with the tactics he'd employed to make certain the woman never came near Daniel again.

**2**

———————

E than Nance. Interesting man. The chestnut hair, dark eyes, lean build...well put together in a blend of style, class, and confidence. But it was the man's brain that was truly compelling...or should she label it mesmerizing? When they talked about analyses and strategies and how they formulated opinions and conclusions, minus the emotion or feel-good parameters most people insisted upon, it was almost like she was talking to herself.

When had that *ever* happened? No need to look too deep because the answer was obvious—never.

Take the intelligence quotient, add quick wit, easy banter, and wrap it all in a guy with confidence, charisma, and style, and he was definitely noticeable. And who would've ever thought he'd subscribe to the same definition of meditation as she did—deep breathing while multitasking?

Yes, they certainly had a lot in common, including Daniel and Meredith.

That's where it got tricky *and* dangerous. Vanessa had sensed the mutual attraction long before she met Ethan Nance in person. Actually, she'd picked up on it after the first phone conversation when they'd been on opposite sides of the Daniel-Meredith situation. Vanessa wanted to protect Meredith from making a bad personal decision that could blindside her and harm the company. Ethan wanted the same for Daniel. But after the big reveal at Daniel's art gallery in Chicago when he told the world he was the man behind Langston Turnings *and* had named his new collection after Meredith? Well, even a non-believer in love and happy endings could see those two belonged together.

Ethan must have seen it too, which was why he sent Vanessa the video clip of Daniel telling the whole world *he* was Langston Turnings and he loved Meredith. The fact that Ethan bothered to get involved said a lot about him as a friend and as a person. That made the man more appealing than his good looks and lingering smile. Perhaps a bit too appealing. Vanessa thought on this as they spent most of the evening together, dined side-by-side, shared a few stories, and discovered they had an awful lot in common aside from their analytical reasoning and belief that a spreadsheet could solve every problem. They also agreed on the absolute need for order and control. And no surprises, ever.

That last one mattered as much as the others. Perhaps more. Surprises relinquished control, destroyed the ability for calculated analysis. And yet, Ethan Nance had been a surprise, or rather the fact that he wasn't the overbearing, overly arrogant man she'd believed him to be was the real surprise. Vanessa hadn't wanted to visit the small town of Reunion Gap, witness the overabundance of joy, stare at all of the couples, so in love, so meant-to-be together while she stood alone. At least, she wasn't the only one alone. She could pal around with Ethan Nance and they could be alone together. There were worse things than spending time with a man of intellect and looks that got a second and third notice.

He definitely possessed charm and knew how to use it, from the smile he gave the proprietress at the bed-and-breakfast, to the casual yet sincere inquiries regarding the type of coffee pot she preferred to her selection of cookware. But Vanessa had seen the shift when he'd spoken of Meredith's father and how the man had tried to destroy good people through blackmail and other nefarious means. There was a hard side to Ethan Nance, but one had to pay attention, look past the cultured voice and designer clothes to notice it. Had that hardness come from experience, DNA, or a combination?

People said there was a hard side to her as well, that she didn't possess the capacity for love or caring about a man. They were wrong. So wrong. She'd trusted a man before, opened her heart, her life, her bank accounts, and the results had been devastating. The experience had torched her relationship with her parents, stolen her belief that love and trust did exist, and crushed her hope that one day she would find it for herself. All of that gone, destroyed because she'd believed lies and trusted the wrong man.

From the few tidbits Meredith shared, it seemed Ethan didn't believe in love or forever either. Had he been hurt, too? Difficult to tell *and* none of her business. What mattered was that she could relax around him, discuss business ethics and office manners without being called odd, *and* could enjoy it because there were no expectations. She didn't *want* a relationship and neither did he. How refreshing was that?

Of course, there was no denying the sizzle when they were around one another, but that was because she'd finally encountered a like-minded person—in intellect and expectation. Truly refreshing. Maybe once this weekend was over and they were back in their respective lives, they could continue their conversations via phone. Or meet up when he visited Chicago. It would be good to hang out with someone who wasn't intimidated by her brains or her confidence.

*Really?* her brain shot back. That's *all* you're interested in? A "pal" to hang out with and discuss business? Not curious what the deep timbre of his voice would sound like when he first wakes up? No interest in running your fingers through that chestnut hair to see how soft it is? And what about those lips? Hmm? No, no, *no!*

Okay, maybe there was a sizzle between them that said *Come closer.* Even, *Let's get closer.* And maybe if she peeled back the layers of denial and resistance, she could admit a *tiny* interest in the man that had nothing to do with his brain. Fine. So, there *was* something about him that made her pulse beat in an I'm-attracted-to-you sort of way. What about it? It wasn't like she planned to act on it. But if she did want to, would he be interested? Well, if the heat in those dark eyes and the extra-long stares were an indication, she'd say there was a strong possibility. Sharing a night with a man who knew the rules of not getting involved and didn't harbor expectations of love and ever-after was not necessarily a bad thing. Was it?

After a restless night consumed with what-ifs and Ethan Nance's handsome face invading her attempts to sleep, Vanessa decided a morning jog would snuff out distractions, *ahem*, namely one man with looks, class, and way too much attitude. Of course, she hadn't jogged in two months, but that didn't stop her from heading out.

Three miles and a much-needed shower later, Vanessa headed to the dining room of the Peace & Harmony Inn, almost wishing she hadn't insisted the owner prepare smoothies every morning. The aroma of vanilla and cinnamon filled her senses, made her wonder if those scents belonged to pancakes, waffles, or muffins and how many calories might be in each. She pushed the thought aside, focused on the calories in her smoothie. Okay, so it might be boring, but it was very nutritious, with lots of greens, and it removed the need for decisions. What was the problem in that? She could calculate the *exact* calories, fiber content, sugars, all of it, and in a world filled with unknowns, at least this was a given.

When she wandered into the dining room, another version of sweetness, a.k.a. Ethan Nance, smiled at her. "You have got to try these." He pointed to a stack of blueberry pancakes smothered in syrup. "I don't think I've ever tasted anything sweeter." The smile spread, landed on her mouth before it shot back to her eyes. "At least not yet."

That was such a ridiculous comment! Totally unbelievable and over-the-top "player" verbiage. And yet, a slow burn worked its way up her neck, settled on her cheeks. Blushing? A man hadn't made her blush in a very long time. Still, when those eyes sparkled and his gaze shifted from her lips to her eyes, his voice dipping just the right amount, it was easy to forget it was a line and not sincerity speaking.

Ethan stood, pulled out the chair next to his. Waited for her to sit. Yes, the man was a gentleman. Another mark for perfection. "Jennifer's fixing your smoothie." He laughed, slid back into his chair. "She even convinced me to try a small sample."

"Jennifer?"

He nodded, forked a piece of blueberry pancake. "Jennifer Merrick, the owner of this place. Nice woman, down-to-earth. We started talking about breakfast choices and she asked if I wanted to sample a smoothie she was making for one of the guests." Ethan lowered his voice as though the table were filled with people and not just the two of them. "I knew it had to be you."

She lifted her shoulder, pretended she wasn't intrigued that he'd thought of her. "You *hoped* it would be me."

He raised a brow. "I did?"

Vanessa blew out a soft sigh. "Of course. So, you could add another piece to my very complicated puzzle."

That comment seemed to surprise him, but he didn't deny it.

"I do love puzzles and I'm quite good at them. In fact, there's never been one I couldn't solve, given time, attention to detail, and good old-fashioned perseverance."

The man thought he could figure her out? Well, he wasn't the only one who could solve an intricate puzzle. Vanessa offered a hint of a smile, leaned toward him, held his gaze. "I'm an excellent puzzle solver myself. My specialty is the person who thinks he can best everyone."

ETHAN HADN'T MADE many miscalculations in his life but thinking he and Vanessa Rodelle could spend time together without a physical "encounter" was foolish and misguided. It was only a matter of time and if he hadn't been so busy trying to show her how clever he was, how adept at puzzle solving, he would have noticed and made the adjustment. But since he'd been so distracted by the woman and *her cleverness*, he didn't adjust anything: not the amount of time he spent with her, not the questions he asked, not how close he stood to her, not how he noticed the scent of her perfume or the shimmer of her lip gloss... And that left an opening for her presence to smother him, snuff out logic, scramble common sense and replace it with red-hot desire.

Fool. Idiot. The truth was that he enjoyed being around her. Her wit and rapid assessment capabilities rivaled his. Her choice of words, speech patterns, obvious intellect, kept him engaged and challenged. When had that *ever* happened? The night he introduced himself at the Alexanders' meet-and-greet, it took her less than three minutes to figure out which guest had invited him to an after-party and which had extended a hot tub visit. In fact, she told him the brunette in the gold tunic dress had been eying him since he walked in and no doubt, he'd receive some form of "invitation" from her before the night ended. She'd been right. *Come share a bottle of champagne with me? Just the two of us...*

How had he not noticed the brunette's direct stare? The way she fingered her low-cut dress in a way that said *You can have whatever you want.* Ethan never missed assessing a room or a situation, but he'd crashed and burned on this one. Maybe if he hadn't been so intrigued with the woman in front of him, he would have picked up on what was happening throughout the entire room. But no, he'd been mesmerized and he couldn't pretend it was just about her brains and wit. There was the face, the body, the laugh, and those full red lips...

Dangerous. Too tempting. Bordering on irresistible.

He should have walked away the second his infatuated brain registered the warning. But for once, he didn't listen. In fact, he muted the warning because since when had he been unable or *unwilling* to control his actions?

Fast forward to the next morning at breakfast, followed by a long walk—he never took long *or* short walks—more talking and a trip to a record store owned by one of the Donovans. Ethan spent all of five seconds in the shop before he spotted the French bulldog barreling toward him. He'd mumbled something about his allergies and rushed outside. Did everybody in this town own a dog? Didn't they realize that not every person wanted to be licked on, brushed against, sniffed?

He hadn't always disliked the idea of a dog. In fact, he'd begged for one when he was twelve, a black Labrador retriever, whom he would name Lucky. His mother should have told him "no", but she could never quite say the word, not when it was just the two of them, and guilt over the absent father sat heavy on her soul. Ethan knew how to play the game and get her to agree by employing only the tiniest bit of persuasion and a wide smile. *I'll walk him, feed him, clean up after him. I'll teach him to play ball, sit and stay, whatever he needs. You'll see, Mom. Please?*

Of course, he'd meant it when he said it and he even kept his promise for two whole months. But then summer came and with it the invitations to swim in his friend's pool, play baseball, go fishing. Lucky just didn't fit into his schedule. The walks and play time shriveled and forget teaching him new tricks.

Lucky, the dog he'd wanted so much, had become a nuisance. He wished his mother had sat him down and had a serious talk about responsibility and honoring a promise. But she didn't because Rebecca Nance never wanted to see Ethan upset or disappointed—especially at her. So, she let him do what he wanted and tried to care for Lucky herself, which was a disaster. How could a person set rules and boundaries when she didn't understand the meaning of either?

After the tragic event that ended Lucky's life, Ethan wondered if the outcome would have been different if he hadn't been in such a hurry to get to the ball field. He might have checked the screen door to make sure it was closed...or spotted Lucky slip through the opening. One extra second of attention, that's all Lucky wanted...to belong, like every other breathing creature. But he hadn't even thought about the dog because he'd only been thinking of himself. When the car tires screeched several yards behind him, Ethan turned just in time to see the sedan strike Lucky. The dog he'd sworn he'd feed and walk and care for died on the side of the road, his black coat smeared with blood, his legs twisted. And every single time Ethan saw a dog, he pictured Lucky lying on the side of the road, eyes glazed, whimpering his last breath.

"Ethan?"

He blinked, forced the images of that tragedy from his brain and focused on Vanessa. She stood two feet away, holding a record album in front of her. "Bob Seger, *Night Moves*." Her face lit up, her voice shifted in awe. "It's incredible."

"Seger gives you a lot to think about, especially regret."

She let out a sigh. "It's as if he knows what it's like to look at your life and wish you could have a do-over. And that voice? Mesmerizing."

Mesmerizing. He liked that word, thought it applied to a lot more than a musician's voice...like Vanessa's eyes...and her smile... And—

"I think you'd be intrigued with Oliver Donovan. The man's very intelligent, but in a quiet way." She raised a brow when she spotted the doubt on his face. "Don't judge a man by his jeans...or his ponytail...or the logo on his T-shirt."

That made Ethan laugh. "Thanks for the advice." He'd heard about Oliver Donovan, and if he were in town longer than a few days, he'd have actually enjoyed a conversation with the man. But the morning after Daniel and Meredith said their "I do's", Ethan was heading out. Maybe he'd try to find a way to get to Chicago next month, see if Vanessa wanted to have dinner, talk about the wedding, the newlyweds, and how they were adjusting to their marital status. Scratch that. Talk of weddings, newly-weds, *or* marriage made his head hurt and he bet Vanessa felt the same. They could talk about forecasts, valuations, marketing data, and profit margins. He bet she'd like that, could probably add a few thoughts on how to showcase a new product.

It was so easy to talk with her; the conversations proved invigorating and he hadn't said that about a conversation with a woman in a long time. But Vanessa Rodelle was different, more like him with her astute observations, sly comments, and on-target assessments. It was quite appealing. Perhaps too appeal-ing, a fact he didn't recognize until it was too late.

## 3

Ethan hadn't attended a wedding in more than twelve years. Some might call it luck or good fortune but it was neither. It wasn't that the invitations weren't extended, because unfortunately they were—en masse. No, the reason he'd been able to sidestep weddings and the associated celebrations surrounding them, a.k.a. bachelor parties, rehearsal dinners, and the like, had to do with his stance on them. *Nothing personal, but I never attend them. Wishing you all the best.* Of course, he always sent an extravagant gift, and that assuaged the hurt feelings and the *Can't you make an exception to your silly rule?*

But a guy didn't blow off his best friend's rehearsal dinner or his wedding, and thankfully, Daniel hadn't wanted a bachelor party. And now, here Ethan stood surrounded by festivities for the soon-to-be Mr. and Mrs. Reese. The rehearsal dinner proved to be a casual affair, filled with toasts, champagne, and glimpses of the happy couple glued to each other as though they really *did* require the other for their next breath. Ethan sipped his scotch, thought about the risk versus reward of giving yourself to another person. Sure, it might be great when sunshine and rainbows filled your day, but what about the second lightning hit and zapped your world? What then? No thanks, not worth it.

Vanessa stood beside him, clasping her champagne glass, gaze fixed on the happy couple. What was she thinking? She'd gone quiet when the toasts began, and had she paled when the well-wishers started tossing out comments like *Made for each other, one and only,* and of course, *forever and beyond?* That might be the mantra for the soon-to-be husband and wife, but Ethan thought of it as sweeter than a square of triple chocolate fudge and just as stomach-jolting.

Interesting that Daniel and Meredith weren't the only couples eying one another as though they really did think the other made their world. There were the Donovans, Rogan and Elizabeth, and Luke and Helena. Ethan spotted Tate and Charlotte Alexander... And the woman with the red hair and designer outfit clutching the arm of a small-built man was a Donovan whose ex-husband was an Alexander. At least he thought that's what Meredith had told him, but it was hard to keep the people and their stories straight. He should have created a spreadsheet, plugged in the names, the connections to one another, including marital status. Spreadsheets were quite effective methods to collect data, even personal data like marital status, number of children, siblings, profession. Maybe he'd talk to Rogan about creating one.

But maybe what he should have done was forget everyone else and concentrate on Vanessa Rodelle and his unwanted attraction to her. They were one of the few *uncoupled* people in attendance, so of course, they were seated next to each other at dinner. Usually, he brought a date to social functions so no one could attempt to attach herself to him. But he hadn't done it this time. There hadn't been anyone on his call-me-anytime list that he wanted to call. That and the fact that he'd been more than a bit curious about Vanessa Rodelle and knew she'd be attending.

The more time he spent in her presence, the less he understood her. Oh, she was polite, witty, even engaging at times, but he couldn't figure her out or break through the barrier of aloofness that surrounded her. A true first for him that made her all the more appealing.

A challenge he could not ignore.

If he'd listened to his head, which warned *Don't be foolish, you're going to get into trouble*, he might have avoided the nightmare that would soon become his life. But arrogance and too much confidence have a way of derailing the best of men when they least expect it. And he would discover that the day after Daniel and Meredith's wedding.

Exchanging vows on the edge of the woods, surrounded by wildflowers, trees, and random bugs would not have been Ethan's first or fiftieth choice, though it fit Daniel. As for Meredith, she might come from high society, but it fit her, too. He guessed it was true that people were adaptable, depending on the situation, the need, and of course, the desire. Ethan wasn't interested in trees, wildflowers, or wooded areas, though there had been a time when he'd actually enjoyed them...but not anymore, not in years.

Vanessa didn't seem to mind. Not at all. He'd caught her gazing up at the trees, lips parted, almost like she'd never seen an oak before. Maybe she hadn't seen one in its natural setting. Not everyone grew up in an area like this and those who did, forgot that some people only saw trees in parks, residential settings, or on television. Those full lips he'd been thinking about for two days pulled into a slow smile as her gaze shifted to a hawk soaring overhead. Either she'd never seen a hawk in nature or she'd seen quite a few. Hard to tell. Ethan's inability to analyze her actions, to determine the motives behind the behavior, unsettled him. It shouldn't be that difficult and yet he couldn't identify a discernible pattern unless he counted the two-second hesitation each time she spoke to him. She hadn't done it with anyone else, just him, and it only started the other day, when they met in person. Now why was that?

He supposed it could mean anything from an attraction to a secret she didn't want him to discover. If it were a secret, given time and a bit more observation, he'd unearth it. On the other hand, what if it were an attraction? *What was he supposed to do with that?* He downed the rest of his scotch, fought the zing to his right temple when he thought about all of the trouble an unwanted attraction to her could cause: a disruption in his routine, his life, his attitude, his sense of calm. *No, just no.*

There was something about Vanessa that made him wonder what it might be like to spend more time with her. Of course, he wouldn't act on it, but he could think about it, couldn't he? He should have steam-rolled that thought the second it landed in his brain, but he didn't and that was a big mistake. Huge. Monumental. A few dances with her, another scotch, more laughter, and his objections to an attraction and the reasons to avoid one began to crumble. He'd caught her staring at him, eyes bright, lips curved into a smile, face flushed.

Why had his addled brain not registered the look that said "interested"? Sure, he'd had a few scotches and it was late, but Ethan didn't need to function at full capacity to recognize a warning signal. He liked to be the one doing the choosing so there was no confusion about what getting together meant or didn't mean—as in, no relationships. But the look Vanessa had given him as he gathered her coat and waited for the shuttle to take them back to the bed-and-breakfast, said she wasn't thinking about tomorrow or the next day.

She was only thinking about tonight.

What was he supposed to do with that? And why did she have to smell so good? Hyacinth and a hint of lavender. A perfect blend of sensual and temptation. Ethan helped her from the shuttle, held the door while she entered the bed-and-breakfast, walked behind her as she climbed the staircase to the second floor, his gaze sliding from her long legs to her hips. Too damn tempting.

He cleared his throat, sucked in three breaths as she reached the top of the stairs. His brain tried to reason with the heat taking over his body. *Don't do it. Don't touch her. Don't do it. You'll be sorry.* Of course, he didn't listen, he couldn't, not when she turned and smiled at him that way, lips parted, shiny, inviting. His brain tried one more time. *Whatever you're thinking is a very bad idea. Foolish. Careless. Unacceptable. Do. Not. Do. It.*

"I'm this way." She motioned toward the third door on the right, began moving in that direction.

He knew exactly where her room was, had figured it out the first night. Why had he felt the need to know where she was sleeping? *That* was another question he'd been unable to answer, not that he hadn't tried.

She removed her room key from her handbag, met his gaze. "Thanks for making these last few days tolerable."

"Tolerable?" Was she serious? He'd call them a lot more than tolerable.

Her lips twitched. "Maybe a little more than tolerable."

Ah, was that was an attempt at humor? Or was the Vanessa Rodelle coolness factor kicking in, making it impossible to admit she'd enjoyed their time together? The woman was as complex and incomprehensible as she was intriguing. At least her refusal to admit she'd had a good time and wouldn't mind more made it easier for him to avoid doing something stupid, like tell her he wanted to see her again, or worse, lean forward and kiss her. Both were absolute "no's" with disastrous outcomes. He should be grateful for the barricade she'd erected with her noncommittal response.

So why wasn't he?

"Okay then. Safe travels back to Chicago." *Back away...leave now...go!* But of course, he had to open his big mouth because Ethan wasn't accustomed to responses that left him confused. "I'm heading there in a few weeks. Maybe I'll see you there." At least he didn't say, *Maybe I'll look you up* or *maybe we'll catch dinner.* Just *Maybe I'll see you there,* which implied an opportunity without a commitment.

"Possibly." Those hazel eyes turned bright and did her lips quiver just the tiniest bit before she spoke? "I hope so."

Those three little words changed everything. Sure, she might fight it and she probably didn't want to admit it, but the truth lay in those words. Vanessa wanted to see him again!

"Ethan, I..." She looked at him, eyes glistening, lips parted.

Waiting? Waiting for him? He hesitated, and then he did something he absolutely knew he shouldn't do. He touched her. Just her hands, but that was more than enough. Truth? It was too much...his fingers slid up her bare arms to cup her face. Seconds later, her eyes fluttered closed and he leaned in for a kiss. Soft, gentle, warm. He should have left it at that, but her whimper shut down reason and before his brain could register what was happening and how to stop it, he'd pulled her against him, devoured her mouth with need and want and desire. So damn much desire. She clasped his arms, held onto him, met the kiss with a passion that unsettled him, forced him to break away. "Vanessa, I…"

He waited for her to speak, say something about what had just happened, but she didn't. At least not with words. Instead, she placed her hands on his chest, leaned on tiptoe and proceeded to show him why sometimes actions really were more effective than words.

"Do you think something's going on with Ethan and Vanessa?"

"No idea." Daniel placed a kiss behind his wife's ear. "Maybe. Probably." Another kiss. "Don't care."

Meredith stepped out of reach, her expression serious. "Daniel, this is important."

He moved toward her, trailed a finger along her shoulder. "And this isn't?" Pink burst on her cheeks, spread to her forehead. No doubt she was remembering his wake-up greeting this morning when he'd—

"Of course, it is." She ran her tongue over her bottom lip, made him think of all the delicious things she could do with that tongue. "But there's something going on between those two and maybe we can help."

Her smile made him almost promise to do whatever she wanted. But poking around in his best friend's private affairs? Regarding a woman? Not an option. Nobody nosed around in Ethan's business, especially if a woman were involved. Had a woman *ever* been involved? He recalled a few attempts by various women, all unsuccessful, all resulting in Ethan's annoyance and claim that people did not understand the words *no* and *not interested in a relationship.* "Meredith. Don't snoop, okay? Ethan won't appreciate it, and he's just starting to get comfortable with you." Pause and a soft "He said you're the best thing that's ever happened to me."

Her blue eyes sparkled. "He really said that?"

Daniel unzipped her dress, eased it from her shoulders, and watched it fall to the floor. She was so damn beautiful...so perfect...and he was so lucky. Too bad Ethan couldn't open up enough to trust a woman *or* a relationship. The man might keep his heart safe, but he had no idea what he was missing. Real love, true peace, endless joy. "Yes, he really said it."

Meredith flung her hands around his neck, pressed her body against his. "Oh, Daniel, that makes me so happy."

He pulled away, stared at her lacy bra and panties. "I'm not sure I like hearing about how another man makes you happy, especially when the guy's my best friend *and* you're half undressed when you say it."

Laughter spilled from her, pulled him in and made him smile. "I love you, Daniel, you make my heart so happy."

She leaned on tiptoe, kissed him on the mouth: long, slow, tantalizing. A kiss of hope, promise, and forever. Yeah, she made his heart happy, too. And he guessed if she wanted to talk about Ethan and potential matchups now and again, he'd have to warn her that his best friend wasn't a relationship or settling-down kind of guy.

"Did you see them talking, heads bent close together? And when they danced? That was more than just a 'share this moment and the song with me'. That was about a lot more."

Only Meredith would try to figure this out on their wedding night. The do-gooder who wanted to see everyone living their bliss. He wouldn't tell her right now that Ethan didn't possess those happily-ever-after sort of emotions, and while he *might* be attracted to Vanessa Rodelle, it would have no staying power. The man believed in minimal fanfare in regard to an expression of feelings from a woman. As for Ethan revealing anything resembling an emotion toward a woman? Probably not. *I don't want a disruption to my state of calm and I certainly don't want to lose focus.* Women tended to do that—big time—and while the rewards were definitely worth it, Ethan wouldn't see it that way. He called a committed relationship a huge distraction, a demand to open his life, his heart, his trust, and even Daniel didn't know why his best friend felt that way.

He'd asked about it years ago, got no closer than *The past served as what I prefer to think of as an education and a time of instruction and hard lessons. Let's leave it at that. Of course, you could hire an investigator to dig around and you'll find answers, but I hope you won't. It will serve no purpose and I'll never be able to trust you... And if we don't have trust, there's not a lot left.* Those words and the expression on his face made Daniel vow he would not pry; he would not investigate and he would not question because he valued their friendship too much.

"So, how do you think we can help get Ethan and Vanessa together?"

Daniel loved his wife more than he ever thought possible, and he'd do anything for her, but he also valued his friend's privacy. "We're going to leave them alone because it's not our business. If they pick up on our attempts to bring them together, and those two over-analyzing strategists will, then it won't be good." He stroked her jaw, brushed his lips against hers. "We have to let nature play out." Another kiss. "Promise me you'll leave it alone."

Big sigh and then "I won't meddle." Her blue eyes lit up with just a hint of mischief. "But can we at least give them an *opportunity* to be together? Maybe schedule a work project where they have to talk and see one another in person?"

"And why would we do that?" The sooner he got his answer, the sooner he could get his wife out of her underwear...

"To let them see how much they have in common as they gaze into one another's eyes, touch hands, breathe in the other's scent...so close...so mesmerizing..." Meredith ran a finger along his jaw, smiled.

"We are not going to encourage them to hook up. Ethan will not be interested in anything long-term and then we'll have a broken heart and the next thing we know, they won't be able to work together and I can't—"

"Husband, we're only going to provide opportunity. Aren't you and Ethan always going on and on about seizing an opportunity when it presents itself? If there's something between them, they'll know, and if there isn't, they'll know that, too. Vanessa is not going to jump into bed with a man she has to work with if she doesn't feel something past the moment."

Well, he hoped she didn't feel *anything* because Ethan didn't possess the emotional capacity to love a woman. At least Daniel had never witnessed it, and he'd bet one of his bowls it didn't exist. "If I agree that we'll come up with a project for them to work on and if it fails, you'll never bring it up again." It *was* going to fail. His observations told him Vanessa was a carbon copy of Ethan: not interested in emotional connections, incapable of committing to another person in a relationship that required give-and-take, opening up, real love.

"Agreed." Her lips brushed his as she reached for his tie. "Thank you."

"My pleasure, Mrs. Reese," Daniel murmured as he unclasped her bra, breathed in her floral scent. He was so entranced with his wife that he ignored the warning in his brain that said Ethan and Vanessa would be a disaster and he'd get pulled right in the middle of it.

# 4

E than woke the next morning to an empty bed and no sign of Vanessa. Her suitcase and toiletries were gone. Aside from a strand of blonde hair on his pillow and her hyacinth-lavender scent clinging to him, there was no indication she'd ever been there.

Where had she gone, and why? There were a few possibilities ranging from picking up coffee, having breakfast downstairs, taking a morning run, to packed up and checked out. Ethan surmised the latter though it didn't take a genius-level strategist to figure that one out. No personal items, no note. Nothing but her scent and that damn strand of hair. He ignored the queasiness in his gut, grabbed his phone and called the front desk. Leave it to a small-town bed-and-breakfast to spill details, including Vanessa's 5:30 a.m. checkout and her somewhat "disheveled" appearance. Hot, steamy sex will do that to a person.

Ethan tossed his phone on the bed, blew out a sigh. Wow, she must have been in a big hurry to get away. So, she didn't want to talk to him, wanted to pretend nothing had happened between them. Well, he'd like to pretend that, too. Oh, yes, he'd like to rewind the clock to the minutes before he landed in her room *and* in her bed, but forgetting he'd touched her? Felt those long legs wrapped around his waist? Heard the tiny sighs and moans? The breathy gasps? Not likely.

Still, he could file the memories in their respectable area along with others he didn't want to think about, smother them if they tried to surface, but not until he understood *why* they'd landed in bed together. The key to a peaceful existence was analyzing situations and behavior, identifying triggers, and setting up safeguards to eliminate potential threats—like a woman who caused him to behave in an irrational and totally unpredictable manner.

With emotion.

Without logic.

Seconds before Ethan made the grand mistake of kissing her, he'd looked into her eyes and the dim lighting made their hazel color appear three shades darker, reminding him of another woman...another time... He should have stepped away—far away —and blamed the desire to kiss her on too many scotches and too many hours spent with meant-to-be couples. He definitely should not have fumbled over an apology and fallen for the sultry look or the nonsense about actions saying more than words. He'd actually fallen for that line? That should have been *his* line if he'd chosen to use a line. But he hadn't, because a fool had taken over his body and that fool wanted to touch and taste Vanessa Rodelle.

That fool had also taken the room key from her hand and unlocked the door. He should not have done that. And following her inside? That was a hard pass, but he'd done it, and he'd done a lot more, too.

Now what? He sucked in a deep breath, blew it out nice and slow. Well, now he had to figure out how any of it had happened.

And why? Was it because for the briefest of seconds Vanessa Rodelle reminded him of the woman who'd owned his heart long before he realized how dangerous it was to care too much?

Or was it something else altogether? Something dangerous and unpredictable?

Last night couldn't happen again and he had to make sure she understood that. Hopefully, she would. Why had she run away this morning? Was she trying to avoid the inevitable *This shouldn't have happened and can't happen again?*

They had to talk about it, even if they talked *around* it because Vanessa was a huge part of Meredith's life and they couldn't just pretend the other didn't exist. There would be gatherings, celebrations, christenings where she'd be present and he didn't want to walk into any of them without knowing how she'd react. He'd always been able to adjust his emotional position based on expectations: but *not* knowing? That would put him at a huge disadvantage and for a man who was a master of anticipating the next move, this was unacceptable. Ethan needed to get in touch with Vanessa as soon as possible and set expectations for future encounters—and make sure she knew what happened between them last night couldn't happen again.

Five unanswered phone calls later, he realized she was not going to return his call. He could confront her face to face when he returned to Chicago: he knew where she worked, where she lived, even the restaurants she frequented. Chasing wasn't his style, and the fact that he had to actually make several phone calls, albeit unanswered, annoyed him. Women usually called *him* several times and *he* was the one who did not return the calls.

*Ethan, I need to see you.*

*I want to see you again. Oh, Ethan, can we talk?*

*I'm available whenever...*

*I'll wait for your call...*
*I'm here for you... Call me... Please.*

And if that weren't desperate enough, there were other more direct offers. *I'm waiting to hear from you... Whenever... For whatever... Just call me. I want to see you...*

It was always the same. The women were beautiful, intelligent, fun, engaging, and none could hold his interest. Why did they feel it necessary to lose their voice and their opinions the second he showed interest? And if he slept with them, why did they think they deserved closet space and the code to his penthouse? Why did they think they deserved a piece of him?

All women weren't like that, and even a relationship-phobic person like him realized that. But the women he selected, no matter the shade of their hair, food preferences, or education level, all possessed one common trait: neediness. Ethan detested the idea of a woman who lacked an independent idea or thought process and selecting ones lacking in that area ensured he would never become attached to any of them.

But Vanessa Rodelle was different. She definitely had her own ideas and she absolutely did not depend on him to tell her what or how to think.

She didn't want to talk to him? Didn't want to see him? He got the message. Why shouldn't he understand it when he'd delivered that same message countless times in the past several years? *Don't want to hear from you. Not interested. Not going anywhere.* Ethan blew out a quiet sigh of relief, forced his brain to visualize water and gentle waves and white sand. Lots of white sand.

Was this a rejection? He hadn't known one of those in years and he wasn't sure he'd recognize it... But maybe it was... Maybe that's exactly what it was. Imagine that?

≈

ETHAN NANCE WAS the kind of man she should avoid. Too good-looking, too sure of himself, way too arrogant. Did he ever make a mistake? And if he did, would he admit it? Oh, she'd known men like him before. They said all the right things, looked at you as though you were the only person who existed, made you believe you were special. And before you knew it, you were under their spell, your thoughts weren't your own but were all predicated on *their* needs, *their* wants. No thank you.

There was no room for another heartache, no room for misguided beliefs or futile possibilities. The only way to get past the night she wanted to erase was to ignore the man. It had been three weeks and the longer she avoided contact with him, the easier it would get, right? That's why she hadn't returned his phone calls and that's why when Meredith hinted at joint projects, Vanessa sidestepped the issue, listed ten reasons why it was not a good idea.

*I don't think we would work well together.*

*We've got different perspectives on the direction to take.*

*Plus, who would be in charge?*

*Do you actually think one of us will let the other run point?*

And then because her reasons for not working with another highly talented businessperson should not be strictly about personality differences, she ended with *This is really not a good time. We've got a lot going on and I don't want to jeopardize our business.*

Meredith seemed to accept Vanessa's objections, though maybe she was just too mesmerized by her new husband to sift through those statements for more information—something that resembled the truth. It was hard to tell, but then something happened that made Vanessa wonder if her friend hadn't been biding her time, waiting for the right moment and the perfect opportunity to revisit her earlier request.

"Daniel and I have been talking about the scholarship programs. He likes what you and I have done with them." A soft smile, a shimmer in her blue eyes. "He says we're truly helping others."

Vanessa nodded, waited for her friend to get to the point. Meredith had a way of talking about feelings and needs and wishes, and by the time she rolled into the real question she wanted to know, the other person had grown relaxed and unprepared for the question. Vanessa had seen it happen many times, and while she knew Meredith didn't do this intentionally, it was a very effective tactic. If Vanessa were a little more touchy-feely, she might try it herself, but that was not going to happen. Those days had disappeared years ago, and an attempt to put too much emotion into a conversation—business or personal—would make her come across as stiff and unnatural.

"So, Daniel's interested in a scholarship program for his company?"

Meredith's smile spread, her voice turned softer. "Yes, he certainly is. Daniel is so kind-hearted. How could I ever have imagined him as cold and unfeeling." The tone of her voice said "in love and under a spell of happiness and forever."

*Maybe because the man lied about who he was and why he just so happened to walk into your favorite café?* Of course, that's exactly what Vanessa wanted to say, but she didn't. Daniel truly loved Meredith and he wasn't a user or a manipulator. But Ethan Nance? He was an open flame that should have *danger* and *highly flammable* stamped on his chest.

"Vanessa? Do you think you can help Ethan set up a scholarship program for their company?"

"Huh? Oh, sure. I'll gather my files and forward them to him." She grabbed her phone, typed a message. "Send Ethan Nance files on scholarship program." It was easier to refer to the man she'd spent one hot and unfortunately unforgettable night with by his first *and* last name—as though she could categorize him under impersonal and irrelevant. If she thought Meredith wouldn't notice, she'd call him Daniel's business partner or the CFO of Langston Turnings or some other nondescript, impersonal title. But because she couldn't risk her friend asking questions, Vanessa forced herself to appear unaffected, definitely disinterested.

Meredith toyed with the tassel on her bracelet, her eyes bright with excitement. She was so full of energy, so in love...so in love with life. Had Vanessa ever felt like that? Maybe for a short period of time back when she was twenty-one and much too foolish. But Meredith Alexander Reese wasn't foolish. She was happy. Content. Doing what she loved and most of all, she'd found someone to share her life, someone who cared about her, accepted her, all of her, including the imperfections. Good for her. People who took the risk deserved happiness.

Not everyone wanted to take that risk, especially if they'd already been involved in a massive fail. Vanessa fit into the "massive fail" category and "not going to step into the risk arena again." What was wrong with being a career person? Taking trips alone? Spending the night reading, or attending a concert with a friend? She didn't need a man; he would only fail her and she couldn't let that happen again. Sure, there'd been a few times when she'd entered into what might loosely be termed a *relationship*, but it had always been with someone who didn't possess her level of intelligence or determination. That approach was safe, acceptable; it was exactly what she wanted.

And then along came Ethan Nance. The aberration she wished she could forget.

How had the man snuck in and stolen her logic and why on earth had she let him? A therapist might be able to shed light on that particular subject, but she wasn't doing that again. No. She did not want to hear about the past and how she had to let it go or how she wasn't the same person anymore because none of it mattered. She'd lost the ability to trust a long time ago. That's what mattered. That's all that mattered.

## 5

Vanessa didn't believe in chance or destiny. And she certainly didn't believe in happenstance or as Meredith called it, serendipity. Serendipity? More like foolishness. There had been a time when she believed she'd find love, along with the picket fence, the children, and the happiness that went with it. But it had all been a lie and the man who'd promised it to her had been the biggest lie of all.

What did a twenty-one-year-old who'd been protected her entire life understand about lies, betrayal, deceit, and the people behind them? How could she have known the man who walked into her life at a friend's birthday party and claimed she was his destiny was nothing but a scam artist whose slick lines were as worthless as the fake Rolex on his wrist? If her parents had let her experience anything close to struggle, discomfort, *anything* that was the other side of "perfect," maybe she would have been prepared. But all she saw in Armand Bernad was a handsome, sophisticated, thirty-something man who knew how to make her feel special.

No doubt all *he* saw in Vanessa was a path to her parents' millions and the prestige behind the family name. It hadn't occurred to her that maybe this new love was more interested in her family name than he was with her. Why would she think that when she'd believed he belonged in their social circles, jet-setting through life, oblivious to cost or consequence? Oh, but the man was handsome, intense, *relentless*. So charming, so well spoken, so absolutely captivating. Three weeks after they met, he declared his love and his desire to spend the rest of his life with her.

*I love you, Vanessa, marry me.*

*I don't care about your money or your family name.*

*I only care about you.*

*I want you, Vanessa.*

*I don't need your money, I need you, with your kind heart and capacity to love.*

*Let me show you how good it can be for us.*

*I'll sign a pre-nup...anything, all I want is you.*

*You're a princess...my princess.*

*Come share my kingdom.*

What he should have said is *You're a princess and I want to be the prince.*

*I need to share your kingdom because I don't have one of my own.*

*In fact, I don't even have a carriage house.*

*And yes, I drive foreign cars and jet set, but someone else always pays for them...usually a woman...never me.*

After, she would learn the harsh truth of believing too much and opening her heart to trust, but it wouldn't come until she'd disgraced herself, her family, and lost her dignity. The Rodelles were well-respected, high-end New Englanders. They had grand plans for their only daughter that did not include marrying someone who was not at least third-generation wealth. When Vanessa introduced them to Armand, they smiled and asked polite questions, but the disdain on their faces showed through.

Even proper, sophisticated people like her parents could not hide it. Armand spotted it, recognized it for what it was—an attempt to save their daughter from a man they deemed unworthy—and that made him even more determined. He sent her family flowers and gift baskets along with personal notes inviting them to lunch, dinner, a weekend at his cabin in Tahoe.

Of course, they declined the invitations and the trip, and that was exactly what he'd planned. For a naïve person like Vanessa, she viewed the rejection as cruel and unconscionable—another of Armand's plans—and that only drew her closer to him. The offer of marriage was a clever one, tucked between "stay strong" and "we'll get through this" along with a ring she would later learn was fake. *Marry me,* he'd said. *I love you. I want to spend the rest of my life making you happy. Say you will. Make me the happiest man in this universe. All I want is you. Nothing more.* Why wouldn't she believe him when her whole world consisted of people who'd told her how wonderful she was, how beautiful, how important? Armand only wanted to love her, and when he looked into her eyes, held her close, and spoke of love and forever, that's all she could see.

If she'd stood back a minute and listened to the spaces between his words, the half second pauses and shifting glances, she would have seen the truth: he might care about her, might desire her, but love? No, what he loved was the status and the money attached to her name. *And* he loved himself because people like Armand always loved themselves first.

When she told her parents she and Armand were getting married, they refused to believe her, and when she persisted, they threatened to sever all financial assistance. *You're still in college. Is your fiancé going to finish paying for the Ivy League education? The condo? And what about the sports car? Does he know you're obsessed with designer labels, or that you've never looked at a price tag?* Vanessa couldn't blame them for their concern, but she couldn't tolerate their refusal to accept the man she loved. Perhaps events would have been different if they hadn't issued the threat to cut her off...but probably not. A woman in love doesn't listen to reason, even when she should. Instead, she listens to her heart, and the man who owns it.

Halfway through her senior year, Vanessa and Armand walked into the courthouse on a Friday afternoon and exchanged vows. No fancy wedding dress, no upscale venue, no bridal dance. No parents. The only witnesses were two of Armand's friends. *We'll have time for a real honeymoon later*, he'd said. *After you finish school and we break the news to your parents that we're married.* The plan was that she would finish school and then she and Armand would move away—Chicago, New York, Dallas—somewhere away from her parents and their over-reaching opinions. *You have to be your own person*, Armand had insisted. *Don't let them tell you what to do or who you can see. They were wrong about me, weren't they?*

She'd never been able to resist that smile or the huskiness of his voice when he spoke to her. And the way those dark eyes devoured her? Oh, but she couldn't think, which was exactly what he'd counted on.

Five weeks into the marriage, Armand bought four shirts, three pair of pants, and a tie for two thousand dollars—with her credit card. When Vanessa confronted him, he'd shrugged it off with a laugh and told her he'd grabbed the wrong card. The smile slipped the tiniest bit, turned firm. *Why the sour face? I'm your husband, you're my wife. We share everything, don't we? Don't worry, once this deal I'm working on goes through, there'll be enough money to buy that house in the Hamptons.*

The house he'd casually mentioned twice, the one she'd never seen. She should have asked more questions, like *What happened to moving away, heading to Chicago or Dallas?* But of course, she didn't because Armand was so sure of everything and she was enraptured by that confidence and take-charge attitude. So, she let him borrow her credit cards, sign her name to a new sports car, even put a deposit down on a boat. Yes, it drained her accounts, but once Armand's deal went through, he'd pay it back. And besides, he was her husband, her partner, her forever.

Vanessa graduated with honors one weekend in late spring. Her parents attended, sat beside Armand, not knowing the secret their daughter had kept from them for months. It all came out at dinner, the moment Armand clasped her hand, raised it in the air, his expression bold, triumphant. *We have more to celebrate than your daughter's graduation.* The boldness pierced their confusion. *Vanessa and I got married five months ago.*

A child never wants to disappoint her parents and she certainly doesn't want to hurt them, but she'd done both. Worse, she'd lied to them, taken the money and support they'd offered and hid the fact of her marriage. It had all seemed justified when Armand suggested it, but it had been wrong and deceitful. The shock on her parents' faces spoke of betrayal and disbelief. And sadness, so darn much sadness. Armand didn't seem to care as he stared at them with a smile she'd later recognize as taunting and informed them they didn't have to support their daughter because he could. However, if they wanted to be part of their family, the one that included children, then perhaps they should revisit their opinion of him and what constituted support.

A piece of her broke that day as she listened to the cruel words spill from her husband's mouth, realized maybe she should not have married so quickly. And children? They'd never talked of children. That was years off. Did she even want children? Did he? Well, eventually, but not at twenty-two years old. Apparently, Armand had other ideas. *We're trying to get pregnant. I don't care if we have a boy or a girl as long as he or she has Vanessa's smile and her eyes.*

What was he talking about? They weren't trying to get pregnant. The stories continued, none of them true, each stripping away another layer of trust, destroying the hope and love she'd once had for him. Her mother broke down and sobbed against her father's shoulder as her father remained stoic, eyeing Vanessa's new husband with pure hatred.

The marriage ended six weeks later, leaving her parents' bank account several hundred thousand dollars lighter, not including the high-priced divorce attorney. But the greatest destruction had been to the relationship they'd once shared with their daughter. It was broken, scarred, irreparable. Just like Vanessa.

*BREATHE. Breathe.* Ethan listened to the sound of gentle waters sifting through his earbuds to reach him. He preferred water sounds associated with rain or a stream when he meditated as opposed to waves. Not that he didn't like waves, because he did... In fact, he'd actually tried surfing years ago when—

*Stop! Focus.* Ethan snuffed out visions of surfing and epic waves, concentrated on the quiet waters with the flute in the background. *Breathe. Breathe.* Was that a flute? Or was it a piccolo? What was the difference? Didn't it have to do with—

*Damn!* He blinked his eyes open, let out a slow breath that had more to do with frustration than meditation. This was definitely not going well. He couldn't even make it ten seconds before his brain jumped to another thought. Ethan placed his phone on the floor in front of him, screen side down. Okay, so this was not the ideal way to engage in a meditative practice but at least he'd removed his shoes and found his way to the yoga mat. That should count for something, shouldn't it? And he'd managed a few breaths, plus he hadn't glanced at his phone, which he usually did while practicing his breathing. *That* was a positive move in the right direction, wasn't it? He'd silenced the damn thing, too. Now that was a big win for a guy who pretty much relied on his devices to navigate his world. Yes, it sure was. Hmm, how many emails and texts had he missed? Maybe the proposal for the—

"I see you're meditating while multitasking again." Daniel stood six feet away, arms crossed over his chest, an amused expression covering his face.

Ethan cleared his throat, tried for a plausible response. "I was taking a quick break." The excuse sounded ridiculous, even to Ethan. How did a person take a break from "taking a break"? Nonsense. "Have you ever attempted to sit still and unplug your brain from the infinitesimal thoughts bouncing around in there, vying for attention?" A slow breath, followed by a shake of his head. "It's much harder than it looks."

His best friend stared at him as though he didn't understand the explanation, or if he did, wasn't buying it. "Infinitesimal?"

Was he laughing at him? The lip twitch and the tone said that's exactly what Daniel was doing. Fine, let the man laugh. "You've obviously never worked to calm your brain." Ethan unfolded his legs from the cross-sitting position, stood and stretched. "I can only determine two possibilities as to why you haven't done it." He grabbed his shoes, carried them to his chair and placed them side-by-side. "Either the creativity found in your woodworking acts as a calming agent and therefore negates the necessity to implement more structured methods such as meditation and yoga, *or* you rely on me to handle your stressors." That sounded reasonable and he'd only thought of it just now. Not bad for "millisecond" analyzing. Ethan stepped into his right shoe, tied the laces. Proceeded with the second shoe.

"You are so full of BS."

Ethan straightened, his half-tied shoe forgotten. "What did you say?"

Daniel's laugh filled the room, landed on Ethan's chest. "I said you're full of BS. When I'm creating, I'm in another world, but that doesn't mean I don't feel stress." He sank into the chair opposite Ethan's desk, crossed one leg over his thigh. "I put a lot of pressure on myself to create the piece I've visualized, and if I'm working on a piece for a client, well, you've witnessed my moodiness. It's because I want to get it as perfect as possible, and that's a huge stressor. You've always been great about taking away unnecessary distractions but that doesn't mean I don't have my own self-inflicted ones."

Okay, maybe. Ethan homed in on the "unnecessary distractions" part. "I just think maybe it's harder for me to decompress because I've always got a lot to manage and my brain refuses to shut down."

Another laugh. "Because you won't give up the control." Daniel gestured toward the yoga mat in the corner of the office. "Five minutes of quiet and you can't do that."

"That's not true." Ethan planted his hands on the desk, leaned toward his friend. "I've gotten to eight minutes, and last week I made it to ten."

The raised brow said he doubted the accuracy of those numbers. "Answer me this; was your phone within reaching distance when you passed this monumental time? Say, *not* in your hand?"

Ethan shrugged. "It was resting on my knee but I placed it screen side down."

"Ah. Was it on silent mode?"

The man knew him too well. "Vibrate," he bit out.

"Wow, look at you. A modern-day yogi in a suit and tie."

"Shut up. Aren't you the one who always talks about effort when I get on you about slow production?"

"Working on a design that's not going well is not the same as refusing to follow the basic principles of a practice, no matter what that practice is." Daniel eyed him. "If you'd ease up on that control you're so obsessed with, you'd start to relax and then you'd be able to sit still without the phone or an encyclopedia of information running through your brain."

"Right." Easy for Daniel to say. Ethan hadn't been able to shut down his brain or his need to control situations in a very long time. In fact, he knew the exact moment and the reason his life changed, and he could never forget it or the woman behind the shift. To do so, would be to dishonor her and what she'd meant to him. But it was more than that. If he loosened his grip on responsible and in-charge behavior, what then? He wasn't about to risk another person's life because he wanted to be care-free. Not doing it. Ever.

"You know, there are more ways to relax than forcing yourself to do it. It's like saying 'don't laugh' and then all you want to do is laugh." Daniel rubbed his jaw, studied Ethan. "It doesn't have to be so structured. Spend an hour or two with those blasted orchids you love." He glanced at the row of orchids Ethan called his "beauties" on the windowsill. "Watch how fast your heart rate slows and you forget to look at your watch. Or redesign your living room." A sigh, a shake of his head. "I seem to recall you were almost giddy with that prospect the last time you did it." Another sigh, a frown. "Don't ever try to drag me to a place with floor-to-ceiling fabric and leather swatches again."

"They were not floor-to-ceiling." The man could be so over-the-top dramatic. "Two racks high, that's all they were. And the leather choices comprised one rack." He recalled that because he'd found the full-grain leather for his couch early on but wanted to make sure it was the best choice. Daniel had mumbled and flipped through samples, commenting on the ridiculousness of so many shades of brown. But Ethan hadn't brought him there to help select choices for his living room. No, he'd asked his friend to accompany him so he could peruse the high-end showrooms and think about how a Langston Turning piece might fit in. If he'd come straight out and told Daniel his plan, the man might have resisted, fearing someone would figure out his identity. No worries there because nobody would suspect one of the premier woodworkers in the country to walk around in faded jeans and an old T-shirt, unshaven and in bad need of a haircut. "Did you forget the real reason I asked you to accompany me?"

"You mean the mega deal you negotiated for Langston Turnings to outfit all five of their showrooms?" The faint smile accompanied the spark in those blue eyes. "I didn't forget, and I'd do it again if you asked me to...even if it was only to look at damn swatches." The smile flipped to a scowl. "But I wouldn't like it one damn bit and I'd probably complain the whole time."

Ethan laughed. "I'll never ask you to do that again. Besides, I think your wife will be the one asking next time."

"Her brother has already offered to help with any decorating assistance. Tate reminds me a lot of you, though I think he's a bit more style-obsessed. Do you know I saw him adjust his tie three times before the ceremony?"

Ethan shrugged. "It's important to get the knot at the proper angle. I've missed it a few times myself."

"There's an *angle* for a knot?"

Big sigh. "Of course there is. It's not spelled out in any how-to manual and there's no mathematical equation for it, though I could easily devise one if—"

"Stop. Just stop." Daniel sat up, cleared his throat. "How did we get on this ridiculous topic? I came to talk about getting the scholarship program for Langston Turnings in place. Meredith says it could change lives and I think it's time to give back." He paused, his voice gentling. "When she talks about the possibilities for this program, her face lights up and I swear, she glows."

*She glows?* Ethan stared at his friend, waited for him to continue. The guy was definitely head-over-heels for his new wife. But did *everything* have to revolve around that woman? Would it ever stop, or please, even slow down? He guessed he understood, but it made Ethan's job more difficult because Daniel's bride didn't always focus on logic or common sense; she depended more on emotions. Why a person would do that when they could rely on data to support the theory, he wouldn't know, but it didn't matter. What mattered was that Ethan had to readjust his thinking *and* his strategies to include Daniel's new wife and *her* thought processes, wishes, emotional state, and "oneness" with the world. Okay, maybe that was a bit sarcastic and overdone, but it had been a lot easier when it was just the two of them, flying solo, with Ethan advising and Daniel counteroffering. It was a business and friendship built on trust, loyalty, and respect.

But now there was a Mrs. Reese who had equal say in her husband's life, and his activities. That proved a challenge, especially when he couldn't gauge what the woman might want, and therefore, what Daniel might want. Wasn't that why Ethan had to reschedule a Chicago meet-and-greet and had gotten dragged into this scholarship program? If he knew where Daniel wanted to end up, he could work his way backward to the presentation, but since he had to factor in the do-gooder wife who wanted to help everyone and disappoint no one, that made his job almost impossible. "So, have you thought about how you want this scholarship program to work?" He should probably just sit down with Meredith and ask *her* how she wanted it to work.

"I have a few ideas, but Meredith thought Vanessa could help."

# 6

----

E than didn't miss the way Daniel's gaze narrowed the tiniest bit or how his voice shifted as though he were trying to gauge Ethan's reaction when he mentioned Vanessa. Ah, yes, the woman who'd spent the night with him and then disappeared as if she'd never been there. Ethan nodded, worked up his most convincing smile. "Sure, just let me know when."

Of course, he didn't mean it, but there was no way he'd let Daniel see just how much he didn't want to reach out to her. It had been five weeks since that night and there'd only been a few stilted conversations between them: three via email, one on the phone. He wouldn't count the text messages or the phone calls that went straight to her voicemail because those were made within twenty-four hours of that fatal night together. And *those* were personal. The correspondence that followed didn't occur until weeks later, after he'd had time to process the fact that Vanessa Rodelle did *not* want to talk to him or see him again—probably at all, but definitely not on a personal level.

It would have been foolish to assume he could pretend she didn't exist, but he could relegate thoughts of her to *strictly busi-*

*ness*. Except that wasn't exactly true. There were too many things that reminded him of the damnable woman: the scent of lavender in the bottle of essential oil he picked up, the leaf he spotted yesterday that was almost the exact shade of her hair… The laugh. The moans that crept into his dreams. The blasted "reminders" proved a nuisance and he'd begun to think the only way to snuff them out for good was to find a replacement. Maybe a brunette, definitely not a blonde, and the eyes should be dark. But the intelligence and wit were key. And then there was the…

*No*, he was not going to hunt for a replacement because that would imply the woman possessed some sort of hold over him, and that would indicate a definite weakness. It was the rejection that had him sidetracked, that and the fact that somehow, she'd snuck past his defenses and made him *feel*. Until he understood the reasons *and* the methods behind them, he wasn't about to engage in anything with any woman.

Two weeks after "the night," Ethan sent the first of three emails. Generic, business centric, beginning with *Hope this finds you well* and ending with *Thanks for your help*. The in-between portion contained an average of six sentences, succinct, impersonal, as though they'd never met or shared more than a casual "hello."

And then there was the phone call. Daniel had asked him to get in touch with her regarding the scholarship setup. The call was Ethan's idea. He'd wanted to talk to her, not about the scholarship, but about why she'd ghosted him. *What happened and why couldn't you have stuck around to say goodbye, thanks for a good time? See you around?* He wanted to hear her voice, listen to the tone and the nuances when she spoke so he could dissect the words and the meaning buried between them. Countless lines of data could be gathered from one simple phone call.

Except nothing was simple with Vanessa Rodelle, including

the phone conversation he'd counted on to make sense of how and why she'd crept into his brain and taken residence there.

*Hello, Vanessa.*

*Ethan.*

*How've you been?*

*I'm well. You?*

*Good. Great. Not thrilled with the below forty-degree temperature, but what can you expect for this time of year, right?* Talk about sounding like an idiot. When had it ever been necessary to toss in a weather comment as a subject of interest? Never.

*Right. We anticipate a heavy frost later this week.*

*I check Chicago weather every day and I saw that. We've already had two, but that's typical Pennsylvania weather.*

Silence.

He was not saying one more thing about the friggin' weather. *So...*

*So, I'm guessing you're calling about the scholarship program. Meredith asked me to send you an outline of how this would work.*

*Thanks.*

*Of course.*

*Okay then... Awkward* did not begin to describe this conversation. His plan to read between the lines and dissect Vanessa's words and tone disintegrated. How did a person do that when he couldn't detect the spaces and the tone held no emotion but a monosyllabic rhythm akin to an electronic voice? *Thanks. Guess I'll see you one of these days.* He should not have said that because it could imply interest, curiosity, even desperation and he was none of—

*Perhaps.* Click.

And then she was gone, leaving Ethan with more questions than he had before the phone call, none of them related to business.

ETHAN NANCE WOULD BE HERE SOON. Vanessa did not want to see him again and she certainly did not want to talk to him about anything business or personal, but she couldn't avoid either. Maybe they should cover the business agenda first and once that was over, she'd address the other matter. But was that really the best course? What if she just dealt with the non-business issue first? Get it out there, put sound to the information that had been living in her head for three days and then move on.

She'd considered keeping the personal matter just that—*personal*—but she'd shared with Meredith and Meredith Alexander Reese had an opinion and a solution for everything. *You can't pretend it never happened. You know that, don't you? Vanessa, tell me that you know you have to have this conversation with Ethan.*

Yes, of course she knew, but that didn't make it easier or welcome. She'd been avoiding the man and trying very hard to pretend that night never happened. Well, she hadn't been successful. Not. One. Bit. Thoughts of that annoying yet irresistible man drifted to her at odd moments: the feel of his hair between her fingers, the smile that gentled his features, the touch that made her believe for one brief second that he might care about her. Then morning had come and with it a stark fear that made it difficult to breathe, propelled her out of the bed-and-breakfast with such force she almost tripped navigating the steps to her car. The flight home proved even more difficult as she envisioned him waking up, finding her gone. What would he think? What would he do? The answers, at least part of them, came via text and several phone calls that landed in her voice mail. *We need to talk. Don't avoid me. We can't pretend this didn't happen.*

But she could and she had, or at least she'd tried. Meredith made the whole pretending very difficult with her intent gazes and curious questions. *So, you and Ethan seemed to get along at the wedding. I spotted you dancing. Daniel said Ethan never talks to a woman when he's dancing and yet he certainly made an exception for you. Interesting, isn't it? Wonder what that means? What do you think it means, Vanessa?*

*No idea.* But typical Meredith didn't take Vanessa's stingy responses as a sign to stop asking. Oh, no, not Meredith. For her, minimal or no response meant keep asking because obviously the other person needed help understanding what was going on. Meredith had gotten better since Daniel came into her life, but she still struggled with the difference between "helping" others and "meddling."

*I didn't see you leave the wedding. When did you leave and did Ethan leave with you?*

There were so many questions buried in there, but Vanessa had been prepared for them. *He saw me back to my room. Ever the gentleman.* Oh, but there had been a few hours when he was not a gentleman...

*Do you plan to see him again?*

More practiced words had spilled out. *I'm sure at some point we'll have to work together, so yes, I imagine so.* But she wished she could avoid him forever.

*I meant on a personal level. Do you think you and Ethan will get together... Say for dinner...the theater...more dancing? He'll be in town, so I figured maybe...?*

Meredith did not give up. *Doubtful.*

*Oh. My mistake. I'm usually very good at spotting attraction, or lack of it, but guess I missed this one. I really thought after watching you two at the wedding...*

Of course, she'd been studying them for signs of mutual attraction. *No. Definitely not.*

But that sort of pretending ended three days ago and that's

when Vanessa had shared the truth with Meredith about what really happened at the Peace & Harmony Inn after the wedding. And how she'd left in the early morning hours, refused the man's attempts to contact her, and tried to snuff it all from her brain.

Except she couldn't.

Vanessa stared at the column on the spreadsheet, but the numbers blurred and morphed into a face with piercing dark eyes and full lips. Why wouldn't he go away? Why couldn't she just erase him? She'd finally settled her brain enough to make it through three pages of financial analysis when Ethan Nance, tormentor and thief of her sleep and oxygen, entered her office and closed the door behind him.

She'd never been good at small talk or pretending around issues. In fact, she avoided issues, preferring to concentrate on unemotional items relating to business, people, circumstances, and situations. Strategies. Analyses. Implementations. This particular conversation would be no different because *she* was in charge.

"Hello, Vanessa."

She sensed him standing on the other side of her desk, waiting. Vanessa dragged her gaze to his, forced a smile. And spoke the words that turned his face to one shade brighter than paste. He opened his mouth to speak, closed it, opened it again.

Ethan Nance speechless? Doubtful the man had ever been left speechless and under different circumstances, she might have enjoyed the reaction. Vanessa shrugged, turned back to her work. "So now you know. Let me just finish this last line item and then we can talk about the number and dollar amount of the scholarships you want to set up. It all depends on your objectives."

She tried to ignore the sputter, the throat clearing, the mumbled curse, but she could not ignore his next words. "You're pregnant?"

**7**

---

**D**o not look up. Keep your eyes trained on the spreadsheet until you're calm. Vanessa picked up a pen, circled a number on the spreadsheet she'd been studying. "That's what the pregnancy test said."

"Pregnant." Pause. "So... I'm the father?"

She wanted to throw something at him. Of course, he was the father. Did he think she was the sleep-around type, hopping into bed with strange men she barely knew? *What else was he supposed to think?* Hadn't she landed in bed with him mere days after they arrived in Reunion Gap? The man hadn't even had to splurge on a meal to get her to bed. No, that had been provided courtesy of Meredith and Daniel's wedding. Not that he would have needed to dole out any money or sweet compliments. Why would he when she'd been so darn willing? So eager? So desperate?

Hadn't she been the one who pressed her body against his, whimpered and moaned like he was her oxygen? What on earth had possessed her to behave that way? Was it because she hadn't been with anyone in so long that she craved a man's touch? And why this man when she had so many other choices, ones who weren't arrogant, self-assured, a bit too perceptive? *Why did it have to be him?* She sipped in air, wished she were anywhere but facing the man who'd given her hours of pleasure—so much pleasure—the kind that embeds itself on a person's brain and body and refuses to disappear.

The kind that left a woman pregnant.

"Vanessa? Answer me." His tone shifted, turned sharp. *"Am I the father?"*

Who cared what he thought or what he thought about her? She didn't need or want his approval, didn't care if he believed her. She wasn't asking for his help...she wasn't asking for anything. In fact, she'd rather he simply walked away. Yes, she wanted him to walk away and leave her alone. But she doubted a man like Ethan Nance walked away from anything until he understood the various facets of the situation, gathered all of the data and extrapolated answers.

*Pretend you're giving a presentation; you can do this. Ethan Nance can't see inside your brain even if he thinks he can. Breathe...breathe...* She lifted her gaze to the too-handsome man, spotted a mix of disbelief, anger, and mounds of confusion. One more breath before she placed her pen on the desk, folded her hands in her lap, kept her voice even. "Contrary to my irresponsible behavior, I'm not in the habit of sleeping with strangers. In fact, it's been a very long time since..." A shrug, a sigh. "It's the only explanation I can find for what happened."

He burned through her with that dark stare. "Well, aren't I the lucky one?" A frown that shifted to a scowl. "Would you have told me if Meredith hadn't commandeered this meeting?" His voice turned hard. "Or would you have waited, maybe not told me at all?"

So, he'd figured out Meredith was behind the push for a face-to-face meeting. Well, he was correct, and now he wanted to know when or if Vanessa had planned to tell him about the baby?

"I don't know what I would've done. I'm still getting used to the whole idea, but I suppose I would have contacted you at some point."

The left side of his jaw twitched, the muscles in his neck bulged, the nostrils flared. This was definitely a man trying *not* to lose his temper. "So, you *did* plan to contact me?"

"I would guess eventually, yes."

More jaw twitching, a cold "For child support?"

"What? No, absolutely not." She held his gaze, spoke the words that would release him from any obligation related to the baby. "I don't want your help." Pause, a sip of air. "I don't want anything from you."

He muttered a curse, dragged a hand through his perfect hair and left pieces sticking up. The proof that she'd upset him was the hair and the fact that he didn't seem to notice. "You don't want anything from me? No money, no help with childcare duties...nothing."

"Correct."

A nod, followed by a shift in his voice that could have been a precursor for anger, disappointment, relief, or all three. "Should I pretend you aren't carrying my child? Maybe pretend there *isn't* a child?"

That would be the easiest... Would he be okay with that? It wasn't as though a child would fit into his life. She didn't know him well, but she sensed that about him and he'd never once mentioned children or family in the conversations they'd had in Reunion Gap. Neither had she, but that was before she learned a child was growing in her belly. That knowledge changed everything, and it made the obvious more apparent; any association with Ethan Nance on a personal level would only complicate her life and confuse the situation. Vanessa could not afford distractions or uncertainties, not when a baby was involved.

She would be mother *and* father to this child, protect him or her and—

"Vanessa, answer me. Do you want me to pretend you're not carrying my child? Maybe dismiss the whole night together as an error in judgment that carried unexpected consequences? Is that what you're telling me?"

How to answer that? The night they shared *was* an error in judgment, no doubt about it, and the look on his face said he agreed. "Look, we can't change what happened. All we can do now is move forward, and that's what I plan to do...on my own." She picked up her pen, twirled it between her fingers, pretended she had a plan. Wasn't it all about perception and image? Let him think this was no big deal...*he* was no big deal. Let him think whatever he wanted as long as he didn't get anywhere close to the truth: he confused her, spun her around, and made her forget why she could never trust a man again. And maybe buried deep down in her soul, a tiny part of her hoped he'd want to be involved in the baby's life—maybe involved in her life, too.

Anger smothered his face, shifted the tan to a dull red. "You don't get to tell me what does and doesn't happen. That's my child, too." He pointed a finger at his chest, glared at her. "My child, Vanessa, not just yours."

The best strategy was always an offense. "What's this really about, Ethan? Control? Trying to run the show and take charge of the situation? Ethan Nance, problem solver to the rescue? I'll save you the time." She pointed the pen at him, steadied her voice. "I don't want your help. I don't *need* your help. I'm very capable of finding my own solutions, and while you might believe your answers are the only valid ones, I assure you, they are not." Vanessa lifted her chin, tossed out more jabs. "I absolve you from any association with me or this child." Oh, he did not like that last comment.

The left side of his jaw twitched, the full lips flattened. The stare burned her. Two seconds passed, three...five... His breath evened out, steadied, and when he spoke the anger and emotion had been replaced with a matter-of-fact calm as though he were delivering a presentation for a prospective client. "I never wanted a child, but it looks like I'm going to have one. That changes everything." His dark eyes flashed. "That child you're carrying is my baby, too. I'm its father and I will not let you try to erase me from this situation."

"Situation? I'm giving you an out. Why don't you take it?"

"Because I can't."

She waited for him to say more and when he didn't, she dove in to change his mind. "Are you saying you want a relationship with me for the next eighteen plus years? Because I'm not going away, so don't think you can strong-arm me or whatever, because you can't."

"I'm well aware that you're part of the equation and that's what I plan to work on...finding out where we fit." He blew out a long sigh, added, "As parents. *Not* as a couple."

"Hardly as a couple." Really? The audacity of the man.

A nod, a clearing of his throat. "Okay then. We should set up a meeting so we can discuss how to proceed. I'll need a schedule of doctor appointments including the location and name of the practice or facility." He rubbed his jaw. "I definitely want to be there for the first appointment...and the first ultrasound. Actually, I plan to attend all of the appointments." More jaw rubbing, a nod. "Have you started prenatal vitamins, yet? I hear there are nutrition books for pregnancy as well as gentle exercise move-ments, calming music and meditation... I'll take a look at your place to make sure it's child-compatible... And I'll definitely have to babyproof the penthouse and—"

"Stop. Just stop." Vanessa pushed back her chair, stood, and delivered the news she'd only now decided upon. "I'm not staying in Chicago. I'm heading back to Reunion Gap to have the baby."

"What? You're going to move there?" He blinked, blinked again, dragged his hands through his hair. Blinked one more time, as though he couldn't comprehend her words or the meaning behind them. "You can't be serious."

"Oh, but I am. Meredith suggested it. She told me her relatives are big on family and a few have babies. She said they'll help me because family is about more than blood." She forced a smile, held it in place until her mouth hurt. "I like the sound of that." If she kept talking, she wouldn't have to think about the coldness of his stare or the way the left side of his jaw twitched. And was he balling his hands into fists? "Meredith has assured me that a single mother would be welcome in this community. I plan to talk to her brother about renting a place. I'll let you know when I make prenatal appointments but obviously, if you're busy I wouldn't expect you to come."

"Get me the schedules and I'll be there."

She nodded, tried to gauge his sincerity, but of course she couldn't. When had she ever been able to read Ethan Nance, either his intentions or his level of interest?

"We're going to have to postpone the scholarship meeting." He glanced at his watch, frowned. "I'll pick you up at six o'clock."

"For what?"

The long sigh spoke of annoyance. Or was that impatience? When he spoke, his voice held a hint of both, along with something else that might be classified as frustration. "To talk about how we're going to proceed, find common ground. Animosity, prejudice, ill will can affect the baby and I won't have it. We're going to have to find a way to get along. The first thing we have to do is get to know each other." His gaze slid from her lips to her breasts, stopped at her hips, inched back to her face. "Aside from the obvious. I'm not going away so don't try any high-handed tactics. You and I have to figure out a way to get along and that might be the most difficult challenge we've ever faced. We're strategists and numbers people, so we should be able to find a formula to accomplish that, don't you think?" He didn't wait for her to respond but nodded and finished with "Pick you up at six." And then he was gone, leaving Vanessa to wonder what had just happened and how Ethan Nance had gained control of the conversation and the situation.

**8**

D aniel had been friends with Ethan for a long time, but he'd never seen the man rattled before. There was a lot going on in that over-intellectual brain of his and Daniel knew exactly what it was... or who: Vanessa Rodelle. The woman had spun him up so hard and fast with a pregnancy announcement, left him floundering, and not even those ridiculous orchids he obsessed over could settle him down.

Damn, but he knew the feeling, had experienced all of it with Meredith when he'd been fighting the attraction, denying he wanted to be with her, and later torn between duty and destiny. Ethan was a brilliant strategist; the man could see everyone else's life as though they were pieces on a chessboard, but he couldn't see his own path. While Daniel had never questioned it, he knew there was something in his best friend's past that kept him from having a decent future...or a real relationship with a woman.

"Are you biting your nails?"

Ethan snatched his fingers away from his mouth, gripped the edge of the chair. "Of course not. I don't bite my nails."

Oh, he'd been biting his nails, another sign of how much a

certain someone was getting to him. "I have nail clippers in the other room if you need them."

Big scowl, a mumbled, "It's a damn hangnail and it's been bugging me."

"Aha. Does that hangnail have a name? Say Vanessa?"

The dark look said he didn't appreciate the comment. "Can you believe she stood me up last night? I told her I'd pick her up at 6:00 p.m. but when I got there, the office was closed and your wife refused to share a personal address." Another scowl. "I hope we aren't going to have problems because keeping information from me is going to be one huge issue."

Daniel sat up, stared at Ethan. "Are you referring to problems with Meredith? Don't try to blame your issues on her. You would have done the same thing if someone I wanted to avoid came snooping around."

"So, you think Vanessa's determined to avoid me?" Ethan blew out a loud sigh. "This is not going to play out well. She's already acting like she's in charge, wants to tell me how things are going to be and what she's going to do as if I have no say in any of this." His voice grew louder, more fervent. "She's having my baby. My child." He jabbed a finger at his chest. "I'm the other part of this equation and I have a right and a responsibility in this situation."

"A right and a responsibility. Hmm, I agree. What's bugging you more? The fact that she doesn't want your help and you think she needs it or is it something deeper? As in she doesn't need you?" That was something Ethan would have said to Daniel and the role reversal showed just how dire the situation with Vanessa Rodelle had become. Had there ever been a time when Daniel had attempted to psychoanalyze Ethan's actions or motives? No, absolutely not—until now. "Talk to me. Tell me what's going on."

"This is not an area I ever expected to find myself in. I never thought about having a child because in my mind that meant there had to be a partner and not just a once-in-a-while partner, but a commitment…a share-the-closet kind." His voice cracked as the next words fell out. "A relationship. And you know how I feel about those."

Yes, Daniel did know but what he didn't know was *why* the man felt that way. Strong feelings like that usually had ties to the past. "I get it; after I lost Sara, I felt the same way. What I'm not sure about is why *you* feel that way." He studied his best friend, spoke the words he'd kept close for too many years. "Something happened that made you that way, and I've never asked because I believed if you wanted to tell me, you would. It doesn't take an analytical genius to figure out you got hurt. The reason doesn't really matter, but whatever happened left you scarred and incapable of committing."

Ethan's expression shifted to one that looked a lot like pain. "Yeah, something like that. Let's just say I'm not willing to take that risk and lose—again. It's not worth it."

"Sure, I get it." So, there *had* been someone in his past. "Are you interested in Vanessa as more than the mother of your child? Because that would be one difficult situation." He thought about the discussion Meredith shared with him last night. *Vanessa said she's used to being on her own and she can take care of the child. She doesn't want to depend on anyone…not when they'll only end up disappointing her.*

"This isn't about whether I do or don't want a relationship with her. This is about how the hell did I get here? I'm going to be a father." His dark eyes grew bright, sizzled. "What am I supposed to do with that?"

"Well, you have a choice, and it's a pretty simple one. Vanessa's not asking for anything. She doesn't want your money and she doesn't expect you to be involved. I'm guessing she won't even put your name on the birth certificate. That's a crystal-clear out. Some guys would take it, no questions asked, no stutter stepping. Or, you could be part of the baby's life. People opt for shared parenting all the time. As long as the mother and father are civil, don't start wars, or use the child as a bargaining chip, you can make it work. But you have to decide what you want and make that commitment, because we're talking about a child, not a number on a balance sheet or an equation. You can't just plug in a formula and run the numbers. This is a human life and you have to respect that."

Ethan dragged a hand over his face, blinked. "I haven't thought about being a father in…" His voice trailed off, he cleared his throat, continued, "I made sure it was not an option, and yet I didn't take the same precautions with her. Why? Why would I not be as precise with this woman as I've always been? What kind of hold did she have over me? What was my lapse in judgment that made me careless and not consider the ramifications of spending the night with her? *What the hell happened?*"

Daniel had a few ideas starting with lust, desire, passion, and good old need. He bet Ethan had met his match with Vanessa Rodelle, and to use one of his wife's favorite words, maybe she was his *destiny*. Maybe there was something about her that made him forget to be cautious, to be calculating, to be in control. The only question now was what to do about it. "I think she got to you and I don't think any woman has been able to do that since the one who broke your heart."

A shrug, a frown, a deep sigh. "I think you're right, but what I don't understand is *why her*?"

"Maybe that's what you have to find out. Get to know her, spend time with her, not in an adversarial way, but in an I-need-to-get-to-know-you way. Maybe you'll even become friends."

Ethan actually snorted and the man never snorted. "Friends? Doubtful. That woman sets me on edge and makes me question everything I thought I knew."

Daniel smiled. "Yeah, sounds about right."

Ethan raised a brow, bit out, "What's *that* supposed to mean?"

"It means when a man and woman are attracted to each other, nothing makes sense. The more you try to fight the attraction, the more confused you'll get. It's like someone's laughing at you saying, *who are you kidding*? But attraction isn't enough in a relationship. If my wife taught me one thing, it's that you have to open up and *share*. What guy wants to do that? I've never met one, but it's what we have to do because it's all part of that package."

"Wait a minute. I am *not* looking for that happily-ever-after package. With this woman, or with any woman. I did that—" he clamped his mouth shut, cleared his throat. When he spoke again there was so much sadness in his voice, Daniel almost looked away. "I did that once… The all-in, open-your-heart, ever-after, want-a-wife-and-children. It didn't matter. It all fell apart and there wasn't a damn thing I could do about it." He looked away, didn't speak for several seconds, so long Daniel thought he wasn't going to say anything. "Let's just say, I don't have those dreams anymore. I created new rules for myself, ones that didn't include long-term or sharing."

And then Vanessa Rodelle entered his life and now she was going to have his baby, and Ethan was stuck between fear, dread, and maybe the tiniest bit of hope. "I'm really sorry. Now I understand why you can help everyone but yourself and why you can't take the advice you give me." His friend's shrug said he agreed and that encouraged Daniel to continue. "You're stuck in a free fall. You can't ignore what's happening. Do you want to be involved in this baby's life? All-in as in changing diapers, doctor's appointments, teacher conferences, homework? Everything?"

Ethan's voice filled with conviction. "I do."

"Okay then." That was a huge step and while the others would be much smaller, at least the man was on a path to answering the important questions. "If I were in that situation and Meredith and I had gotten pregnant early on, what would you have told me? Think about it and tell me exactly what you would have said."

Ethan sipped his scotch, cradled the glass between his hands. "I'd ask you the same question about the baby and if your answer was that you did want to be involved, then I'd move to the second part of that equation. I would tell you that being involved with the baby did not necessitate an intimate relationship with the mother, but I would ask if you wanted one." He pinched the bridge of his nose. "If you said no, I'd let it go. However, if you indicated you were interested in something more personal that went beyond the parent role, I'd ask you to qualify that statement." A smile slipped out, spread. "You wouldn't like that comment and I'd expect a few curse words, but it would get you thinking."

Now they were getting somewhere. "And how would that look? Give me the next steps in the scenario."

"Again, it's a simple formula and a path. I would say you might not know what you wanted yet and would advise you to spend time with her to identify the relationship. What comprises it and to what degree? If it's solely parent-to parent, then your approach would be geared toward coordinating all aspects of care for the child, including physical, educational, emotional, etc. You get the picture."

"I do." Talk of plans and purpose and the implementation of strategies had relaxed Ethan, and maybe this "relaxation" would uncover a few things about *his* goals and wishes he hadn't considered. The key was to keep him talking and eventually the answers would spill out. "And if it's not just a desire for a parent-to-parent relationship?"

Ethan drained the rest of his scotch, cradled the glass in the palm of his hand. "Then you've got a whole other situation, one that requires more strategies, caution, and razor-sharp observation. It's much trickier when emotion gets tangled in the information-gathering process, and it can corrupt the data."

"Corrupt the data?" Daniel stared at him. "Are we talking about a computer or a person?"

Ethan ignored the sarcasm, went on to explain. "When the brain is seduced by emotion, it sees situations in a different light. Think of a camera whose lens has been blurred. You lose visual acuity." He blew out a long sigh. "You think you're looking at a cloud when in fact it's nothing more than a smear on the lens."

That was an interesting visual, bizarre but interesting. "So, are you saying Meredith and I are destined to live our lives out of focus?"

"No, just the opposite, though it might appear that way in the beginning. The inability to focus and find clarity occurs in the discovery phase. Think of two people who are attracted to one another. They may or may not acknowledge it, but eventually they'll have to admit the attraction or move on. Both are acceptable choices, but both have consequences."

"Can you just explain this in a simple-man's terms without dancing around about consequences and choices?"

Ethan ignored the commentary, continued as though he hadn't been interrupted. "If a person is interested in the possibility of a deeper emotional attachment, a.k.a., a couple, he'd have to consider compatibility factors, similarities, willingness to compromise, what constitutes game changers as well as deal breakers. All of that and since we've worked together so long and have been friends even longer, you have a good idea what those are."

*Exactly.* "Do you realize you could employ these tactics for yourself and *your* situation with Vanessa?" Daniel studied Ethan, waited for the guy to reason his way out of his own logic.

"Me?" The dark eyes flashed, the lips flattened. "I strongly doubt I could make the all-in commitment."

"Maybe, maybe not, but I saw you two together in Reunion Gap, and I remember how interested you were to talk to her long before there was ever a face-to-face meeting. I can't think of a time when you actually looked forward to talking to a woman, especially one you'd never met."

Long pause. "I found her intriguing...a cerebral challenge."

Daniel raised a brow. Sure, he'd go with the whole cerebral intrigue or whatever the guy wanted to call it, but there was also something else there and Ethan must have sensed it long before the face-to-face. Attraction. The kind that shot from the brain to the crotch, circled back and consumed a person with desire. Ethan wouldn't like admitting that one so Daniel side-stepped that comment with "She's still the same person, and if you both step back and stop trying to best each other, who knows what could happen? Shouldn't you give yourself an opportunity to find out? You two may not be compatible once you spend more time together. You may just co-parent and then you'll have to decide how that looks." Daniel rubbed his jaw, slipped in the other possibility. "Or you'll realize you want a lot more than a co-parenting gig and that's going to scare the hell out of you. Of course, it's not just about you...you'll have to see if she feels the same way." Ethan in a state of uncertainty? Now that would be something to see. Daniel hid a smile. "I'm sure you wouldn't look forward to that."

"Are you saying if I offered more than co-parenting, she might refuse?" Ethan laughed as though that were an impossibility. "You really think she'd say no to the commitment and the whole until-death-do-us part? With me?" Another laugh.

Oh, but this man had a lot to learn about falling for a woman who wasn't exactly anxious for his attention *or* his affection. It was going to get interesting… Downright explosive… "Don't know, but maybe we'll find out. Let's not get ahead of this whole situation. Why don't you plan it out and strategize like you do every other aspect of your life and you'll be fine. The answer will come and it will be very obvious."

"Are you using my tactics on *me*?"

"Guess so." Daniel grinned. "They worked on me, didn't they?"

"Of course they did."

"Just don't do one thing."

"What?"

"Don't sleep with her again until you know which direction you're heading. Don't do it; take that from a guy who should've listened to your advice and didn't." He'd almost lost Meredith, the only woman he'd ever truly loved. He should not have touched her until she knew the whole truth about who he was and why he'd sought her out. But of course, common sense and logic didn't often play into any equation when desire and passion stepped in their path. Ethan might think he could control every aspect of his life, including the emotions he kept buried, but Daniel's gut said Vanessa Rodelle might be the one woman who could change that.

# 9

Three days after she'd told him she was pregnant *and* no-showed for the meeting he set up, Ethan appeared. At her office. During business hours. And now he sat at a worktable in the common area with papers spread out in front of him. He had printouts, calendars, and good heavens, was that a power-point presentation labeled "Baby and the Future"? The man was over-the-top ridiculous and if he thought he could control *the situation* as he called it, well, then—

"Vanessa. Hello. Thank you for agreeing to meet with me." He cleared his throat, pointed to the papers in front of him. "I spent the last few days collecting data and gathering information I think will help us. We both find comfort in numbers and do better with analyses and projected outcomes than a feeling or a guess. Given that, I think we have a fair chance for success if we follow protocol."

"A baby is not a projected outcome, Ethan. He or she is flesh and blood and trying to make it anything else is unrealistic and short-sighted."

Red splashed his cheeks, and he stumbled over his next

words. "Absolutely. I get that. I'm just trying to put the framework around this so we understand it."

Oh, but the man did seem rattled and out of his usual "cool" zone. "I'm comfortable, or as much as I can be considering these next several months will stretch my body, leave lines and veins and who knows what else? But it will be worth it, no doubt about that." She'd never much considered the physical and emotional upheaval pregnancy created because she'd never thought about being pregnant, though she'd assumed it would happen one day. But that was years and a marriage ago. When the marriage ended, so did the vague notion that she would one day be a mother.

Now here she was, pregnant, unattached, but oddly *not* petrified. Her gaze darted from Ethan Nance's flushed cheeks to the unsettled expression clouding his face. What was he really thinking? What was his plan? She'd given him a way out and he'd refused. Why, that's what she wanted to know. "Why are you really here? I thought you would've left Chicago by now."

The red on his cheeks shifted to maroon. "I'm taking care of business here and I'm not finished yet."

Vanessa sank into the chair opposite him, folded her hands on the desk. "Business? Langston Turning business? Scholarship business?"

He looked away, blinked, and shifted his gaze back to her. "Neither. This was more important and required my undivided attention."

Why did he have to look at her that way as if he *cared*? Vanessa fought the jumble in her belly, attributed it to the pregnancy even though she hadn't experienced any morning sickness. She cleared her throat, pretended she hadn't noticed the dip in his voice or the lingering gaze or the way he—

"I brought you some tea." He removed a brown bag from his briefcase. "It's green tea, loose leaf, decaffeinated. I wanted to get you something and this seemed like a good choice for you and the baby." Big sigh and a frown. "However, after I bought the bag, I wanted to do a bit more research and that's when I landed on pages that talked about how green tea could affect the absorption of folic acid and you need that to avoid neural tube defects. One article led to ten and I almost tossed the stuff in the trash, but then I read a few more articles and decided we should hang onto it and just ask the doctor at the prenatal visit." A shrug followed by an uncertain "So, if you wouldn't mind, can you wait until the first visit so we can get clarification on the tea?"

Wow, talk about being concerned and sensitive! Vanessa could ignore the comment or pretend she didn't appreciate the gesture, but why, other than to be flat-out insensitive? He'd just shown her pure kindness and she *did* appreciate the gesture *and* the effort. "Thank you. I think it's a good idea to wait for the first doctor visit." She accepted the bag, read the description, smiled. "I'd like to hire this person to do my marketing. 'Calming as a gentle waterfall...' Very persuasive and quite tempting. I'll bet they convince tea haters to reconsider their stance."

That made him smile. "There were so many to choose from and I only looked at the decaffeinated ones. I read all of the descriptions but after a while..." The smile spread, followed by a shrug. "I'm as gullible as the next guy when it comes to being pulled in by the marketing. Who doesn't want to sample a communion of bliss and quiet? The salesperson insisted this was the one, 'not to be ignored.' But if it's not, I'll head back there and tell him we want to 'ignore' this one."

She didn't hear much after he admitted he'd pondered several descriptions in an effort to select the perfect one. And how many articles had he read about green tea and pregnancy? A ton! That must have taken quite a bit of time and Ethan Nance did not appear to be a time waster, which meant he didn't consider tea hunting or researching tea drinking while pregnant a waste.

Something deep inside her softened. "Just because I plan to wait on the tea doesn't mean you should. Would you like me to make you a cup?"

He hesitated. "That doesn't feel right. If you aren't drinking, neither am I."

She raised a brow, clutched the tea bag. "Are we only speaking of tea, or might you be referring to other drinks—say, ones that contain alcohol?" Vanessa had been joking and expected a laugh from him. What she did not expect was his answer.

"I've decided to forgo alcohol for the duration of the pregnancy." His voice dipped, his expression softened. "It's the least I can do."

"Oh. Well. Okay." She wanted to ask him why he would do that but held back. Ethan Nance seemed different from the last time she saw him. More approachable, more appealing.

And that could be a very big problem because the man did not and could not fit into her life in any way other than as the child's father.

How had everything gone so wrong so fast? He and Vanessa had been enjoying a civilized conversation up until a few moments ago, one that included laughs and more than one smile. Of course, he'd spent way too much time talking about green tea and his mission to find the perfect one, but she'd seemed intrigued, maybe even touched by his efforts.

And then he brought up the subject of relocating to Reunion Gap during her pregnancy. The idea had been on his mind since she first mentioned it, but he'd planned to wait until they were on better "talking" terms to ask her to reconsider. It was all about timing and the slow approach, especially with Vanessa. He thought the plan made no sense and was definitely driven by emotion, rather than logic. Or the pregnancy hormones were already kicking in, creating over-the-top reactions to logical choices.

Why would she want to leave Chicago when there were premier hospitals, specialists, support groups, all of the necessities and amenities for babies and new parents? Hadn't he just read about a play group for first-time parents? Why wouldn't she want to take advantage of that? All she had to do was agree and he'd set it all up.

But no, Vanessa Rodelle was not interested.

"There are good doctors in Reunion Gap. Meredith said her relatives have recommendations and they're happy to share. What better situation than to be among people who have children and have gone through it? I don't know many women with children, at least not on a personal level. Do you know any men you'd sit down with and ask about the delivery room experience?"

"No, but I wouldn't ask anybody personal questions like that." Ethan grabbed his water, took a healthy drink. Why had he spouted off about giving up alcohol during the pregnancy? Talk about impulsive and not well thought out. What a foolish idea. Why had he done *that*?

A laugh, followed by an amused "And that's the point. You're unwilling to expand your comfort zone and reach out to people who might be able to help with this whole process. The more we know about what to expect, the easier it will be."

Easier for whom, he'd wanted to ask. And speaking of easy, it would have been easier to have this conversation at his home or hers, instead of the worktable of a cramped office surrounded by file cabinets, stackable bins, and poster art about positive thinking and imagining the impossible. Ethan forced a smile, determined to explain his reasoning for trusting himself as opposed to outsiders. "If someone has information or something to say that could be helpful, then I'd consider it. But I'm not going to listen to every fly-by-night who comes through with an idea or a thought just because they've popped out a kid."

"Popped out a kid? What a pleasant visual."

"Okay, I didn't mean that." He cleared his throat, tried again. "Sorry, that isn't what I meant."

"There really is no way to have a normal conversation with you, is there?"

"You mean a conversation where I have to agree with you, even when I don't?"

Those hazel eyes sparked, burned him. "You, Ethan Nance, are not an expert in everything. The high IQ and the ability to solve complex puzzles and use big words don't make you an expert on pregnancy or childbirth. I'm going to Reunion Gap and that's where I plan to have the baby, so if you're interested in that, fine. Come to Reunion Gap or don't. Visit for the baby appointments or don't. I told you before, I don't need anything from you and while I appreciate the prenatal books and the green tea, I can handle all of it on my own."

"And that's it? You're packing up and bailing out?"

The full lips flattened, the tiny nostrils flared. "No, I'm packing up and relocating, and whether it's temporary or permanent remains uncertain. I'm going to see how things play out."

That was definitely an emotional response. "What does that even mean?"

"It means just that. I'll see if I'm comfortable there, if I adapt well, if I miss Chicago. I'm starting to realize life is about more than the next client. Maybe if you ever got out of your need for order and planning, you'd realize it, too."

Ethan sighed. "You are one difficult woman."

"Thank you." Her chin jutted up, followed by a frown. "You are one stubborn man."

"Do you have a place to stay or are you going to see how things play out with that as well? Ride in and take a chance there's a vacancy at the bed-and-breakfast or the Alexander mini-mansion?" No doubt she'd already figured it all out and just neglected to tell him.

"I said I'd see how things go; I didn't say I was foolish. Of course, I have a place to stay, and of course, I've got a plan."

"Care to share?" The woman infuriated him.

"For now, I plan to stay at the Peace & Harmony Inn, or I might move to one of Tate Alexander's rentals. He's offered, but... We'll see. I think I'm more comfortable at the bed-and-breakfast for now."

"The memories there won't be a problem for you?" *The hot steamy sex? The moans and sighs of pure pleasure?* He should have kept his mouth shut, but it was too late to pull back the words or the visuals stuffing his brain. His comments didn't garner any reaction: not a blush, a snarl, a curse, nothing. No woman had ever unsettled him the way this one did and it absolutely drove him crazy. Not in a good way. He needed time to figure out why this was happening so he could shut it down. Ethan would solve the very complicated, convoluted puzzle of Vanessa Rodelle, no matter how long it took. For now, he just had to keep his wits about him. He could do this. One breath, two, three and a calm "I'll see you in Reunion Gap."

## 10

E than had been in Reunion Gap four days, living in the rental unit Tate Alexander found him.

*It's a bit rough*, Meredith's brother had said. *But maybe you can make do until Luke can send a few guys over for repairs.*

He meant Luke as in Luke Donovan. That would be Tate's brother-in-law. Charlotte was Tate's wife and Luke's sister. Daniel had tried to explain the people and their relationship to one another, but it would have made more sense if he'd had family trees and a reference guide. How many Alexanders and Donovans were there? And what about the monster himself, Harrison Alexander? Ethan planned to dissect and learn everything he could about the man who'd almost destroyed Daniel and Meredith's relationship.

He set down the sander he'd bought this morning. It would make prepping the cabinet doors for painting so much easier than sanding by hand. If the hardware store had the sander in stock, he would've picked it up when he got the other power tools. The cordless drill sure made removing the cabinet doors quick and easy. And the power miter saw would be great for achieving an accurate cut for trim and molding. As for the battery-powered nail gun? Nothing like having something fast, efficient, and fun to use.

This place needed a lot of repairs: the sink and vanity in the bathroom; ceiling fans in the bedrooms; outdated lights, switches, and outlets; new baseboards; and door frames throughout the house...and paint...lots of paint. And there wasn't a working dishwasher or garbage disposal. Ethan hadn't thought about repair work or carpentry in years, but once he walked into this house, something happened to him. He *wanted* to pick up a hammer, tear out old molding...fix and create.

If Daniel dropped in before Luke Donovan sent his crew over, how would Ethan explain the repairs? As far as Daniel knew, Ethan didn't know the difference between a circular saw and a seesaw, much less how to use one. It wasn't that he was trying to hide his past from his best friend; it was that he didn't like the reminders of the work he'd had to do to help his mother. No father, no steady income, nothing but ambition, and a mother who insisted on spending all of their money on him. She'd never quite figured out that what he really needed was guidance, a firm hand, and honesty about their financial situation. *We don't have the money for you to attend summer camp. You'll have to settle for the less expensive jeans. Sorry, but we're on a budget.*

But no, Rebecca Nance didn't say a word because she believed he deserved only the best, no matter what. He'd been fifteen the first time the electric got shut off, followed by the phone a month later. That's when he began to notice the past due and collection bills piled in a cabinet above the coffee pot. There'd been so many of them! Ethan had grabbed them and spent the next few hours creating a spreadsheet and a plan to get his mother out of debt. When she came home from her job at the clothing store, he'd presented her with the spreadsheet *and* a plan. She'd insisted she did not need his help; *she* was the mother, she was the one who should provide for him.

Sadly, she couldn't because her belief in what constituted the meaning of *provide* was skewed. That's when Ethan realized he'd have to take over as the responsible member of the family, but he'd have to do it in such a way as to make his mother believe *she* was still in charge. It worked and it didn't work. When he found an after-school job with a handyman, she didn't fight it, but she also didn't stop spending money on him.

His mother never understood the concept of money in or money out. Debit. Credit. She certainly didn't grasp the concept of saving. Ethan hadn't held a hammer in a long time and the only things he'd built in years were spreadsheets. While he'd fought the sawdust in Daniel's shop and tried to run from the memories of those days, there had been a certain satisfaction in repairing, creating, even repurposing.

What did he do now, other than buy, discard, and buy again? The latest, greatest, most technologically advanced, highest thread count, designer labels? None of it made him happy… Not for long. And that's why the feel-good approaches like yoga and meditation had become part of his daily routine, even though they were half-hearted attempts with frequent interruptions—of his own making.

But these past few days when he'd been working with his hands, building a temporary workbench, removing the kitchen cabinet doors to prep for painting, actually sweating from physical labor instead of exercise classes, he'd found a certain peace he hadn't felt in years. Last night he'd dropped onto the bed, exhausted, definitely sore, but satisfied with the work he'd done that day. Calm. Content. Achieving a goal he could see and touch had its own rewards.

Maybe there was a reason he'd landed in Reunion Gap. Maybe it was so he could find himself. Ethan contemplated that possibility and the ramifications of it as he replaced a light fixture in the kitchen. His world had changed in ways he could not have imagined and certainly not planned for, but he was done anticipating every step, especially where Vanessa was concerned. She was a mercurial force he could not understand or control, and he would have to find a way to accept that.

When the doorbell dinged a short while later, Ethan thought for a half second it might be Vanessa. Logic told him that was an unrealistic possibility, but it didn't stop him from wondering. He placed the tape measure on the workbench, made his way to the front door.

Tate Alexander stood outside, a bottle of top-shelf scotch in his hands. "Thought you could use a drink."

He could certainly use a drink, but he'd made that stupid vow to give up the stuff during Vanessa's pregnancy. "Thanks." Maybe Tate wouldn't expect him to open the bottle during his visit. That would save Ethan from answering a lot of questions he didn't want to answer. "Come in, you can check out what I've been doing."

Tate stepped inside, shrugged out of his coat, and didn't wait to comment on Ethan's jeans and T-shirt. "Call me naïve, but I had no idea you owned an old T-shirt, much less one with paint on it. And the jeans?" His silver gaze took in the faded jeans. "Not unless they were designer label, preferably dark-washed."

Ethan shrugged, fought the heat rushing to his face. "Pick the appropriate clothes for the job at hand." Another shrug, a grin. "I didn't think royal oxford shirts and wool pants were appropriate attire for plumbing and carpentry."

"Point taken." Tate followed him into the kitchen, stared. "What happened to the cabinet doors?"

"Yeah, about that... They're in the basement in paint prep. They were pretty beat up and it's an easy fix to give them a facelift. I also plan to paint the cabinet fronts. Again, easy enough to make a big improvement."

"I see." Tate studied the cabinets, nodded. "Luke offered a painter and a few other trade guys to straighten things out for you but it looks like you don't need their help." He eyed the new light fixture above the small table, his gaze sliding back to the cabinets. "Actually, it looks like you don't need anyone's help. Hmm. Does Daniel know about this particular skillset of yours?"

"You mean that I can balance a spreadsheet *and* use a hammer? No, and I'd appreciate it if you didn't tell him. If the guy knows I have other talents, he might try to put a hammer in my hand and I'm not especially fond of dust."

Tate nodded, said in a quiet voice, "I get it. Our past and what we've done there shouldn't define who we are or what we do now. Daniel won't hear a word from me."

"Thanks."

"How about we toast on our plan to keep the past where it belongs? I'm pretty sure there are a few glasses in the cupboard, but I can't guarantee the ice cubes."

Ethan tried to think of a response to explain a decision he didn't really understand himself. He cleared his throat, let the truth spill out. "I like my scotch neat, so the ice cubes aren't a problem, and that is definitely one of my favorite brands."

"But?"

"But for some ridiculous reason I can't identify or qualify, I gave up drinking until after the baby comes."

The man smiled, and not just a half-smile either. "I see."

"Yeah, not one of my most calculating moves." Big sigh and a scowl. "Open the bottle and have a drink for me."

Tate ignored the request, homed in on the previous comment Ethan made about not understanding why he'd given up alcohol during the pregnancy. "Maybe you can't figure it out because it's more heartfelt than calculating, ever consider that?"

"No." *No!*

A shrug, another smile. "Give it some thought. You might be surprised when you stop fighting the possibilities." He handed the bottle to Ethan. "Why don't you save this until the baby's born? Then we'll break it open and have a real celebration."

There was something about the man that let Ethan relax around him. They'd only had a few conversations, but they seemed to share a lot of the same interests and not just fashion or business. He liked the guy's straightforward candor, the willingness to take charge of a situation, the no waffling, no taking sides, no second guessing. Pretty much like Ethan. The guy had heart and a soft side he didn't mind showing or sharing, and that's where he and Ethan were very different. Ethan was a master at burying feelings, especially ones he didn't want to acknowledge or address. He'd been that way for too many years and chances were he'd never change.

There was a reason and she even had a name.

Darcy Pennington.

Life had a way of making its own path just when you thought you had it all figured out. It didn't matter how careful you were, how well constructed and detailed the plan, or how much you wanted to succeed. That last one really didn't matter because when life or fate, as some called it, crashed your world, you never saw it coming.

It just happened and then it was over and you were left to sort through the mess of what used to resemble your world. Only you couldn't recognize it any longer because the one person who belonged in that world, the one who made everything matter— was gone.

That's what happened to Ethan Nance and Darcy Pennington late one summer afternoon thirteen years ago on a country road in Pennsylvania, surrounded by trees, sun, and the promise of forever. Ethan had patted his jeans pocket containing the velvet box, thought of the words he would speak when Darcy arrived. *I love you. Will you marry me and be my forever partner?* If she'd driven instead of insisting on riding the damn bike, the events would have been different.

Life would have been different.

But he'd never been able to convince her that sometimes logic and common sense really should beat out *It's what I want to do*. Ethan had checked his watch, calculated how long the four-mile ride would take, squinted at the winding road. If she left at the designated time, she'd be here in ten minutes...the place of their very first kiss. Another ten minutes and they'd be engaged and planning their happily-ever-after.

Except that didn't happen. Not even close, because on that perfect, hope-filled day, Ethan watched the only woman he'd ever love emerge from the curve in the road, covered in sun and a smile that almost blinded him. He'd been smiling too, arms outstretched, waiting to pull her into his arms and promise her forever.

After, he wondered if she heard the car behind her, or the screeching brakes as the driver sent her flying over the guardrail to the rocks below. Darcy Marie Pennington, the love of his life, the woman he'd planned to marry, died that afternoon. She was twenty-one years old, and nothing could save her: not prayers, not destiny, not Ethan's love. But on that day, Ethan's belief in true love, forever, and always died, too.

# 11

---

Ethan Nance was one persistent man. He'd followed her to Reunion Gap, rented a house from Tate Alexander, and word had it Ethan was having the place remodeled as though he planned to stick around for a while. But with a person who demanded order and a pristine environment, Vanessa bet he'd want a remodel done even if the stay were short-term. The man wouldn't care who he pushed out of the way to get the work done as long as he didn't have to wait. Tate should have told him if he wanted work done, he could either wait his turn or do it himself. That last possibility made Vanessa smile. As if the man had ever held a hammer in his hand or could identify different types of screwdrivers.

She'd only seen him twice since she'd told him about the pregnancy. Once at her office when he'd brought her tea and a "baby presentation" complete with calendars and schedules. The second time was a few days ago, when she first arrived in Reunion Gap. He'd been at The Oak Table, a restaurant run by the husband of Meredith's close friend. Vanessa had caught Ethan's profile sitting at the bar—movie-star good looks and old-money class—chatting with a dark-haired woman. Not just chatting either, but laughing, smiling, lots of smiling. And drinking? She'd eyed the glass in his hand, frowned. So much for not drinking until the baby came. The man always had a line and while he might believe his words when he spoke them, the promise no doubt fizzled five seconds after it left his lips.

Not surprising.

One more look at the dark hair, the firm lips, the tanned hands... Vanessa had turned and left the restaurant before he saw her, ignoring the ping of disappointment surging through her. This was why she could not let the man into her life other than as the baby's father. *Could not even consider it.* The man was a player and had already spotted his next target. A pregnancy was not going to keep him from an attractive woman. Not her business. She did not care. But there'd been a few times during their last meeting when she'd caught him watching her a bit too closely, as though he might be interested in her as more than the baby's mother. How could that possibly be true? A man like that would never settle down with one woman, even if she were carrying his child. Only a fool would believe otherwise and Vanessa was done playing the fool for the men in her life.

*Men in her life?* Ethan Nance was in her life by default, not choice, and if she could figure out a way to get rid of him, she would. The move to Reunion Gap hadn't done it, though she'd thought it might. A playboy businessman like that wouldn't find comfort or pleasure in a small town the size of a convention center. He'd grow tired of it, maybe once he realized that no matter how many updates he made to the small Cape Cod he'd rented, it was still not the penthouse he was used to... What sort of remodeling was he doing and what was the real reason? Had he convinced Tate that renovating the place was a sound, long-term investment?

Too many questions swirled through her brain, leaving her

with more confusion and less certainty regarding the man's true motives.

At least she'd found a snippet of serenity in the Peace & Harmony Inn and Jennifer Merrick was a big reason behind that. The woman was a good listener with a compassionate tone and a look that encouraged a person to share. Vanessa was not used to sharing, hadn't done it in years, and yet she found herself telling Jennifer about her predicament.

There'd been more than a few curious glances when she entered the Cherry Top Diner, walked along the main street, sat in the park. Meredith told her that in a town as small as this one, people noticed the comings and goings, the interactions that occurred between people. Vanessa guessed there was a certain comfort knowing you could turn to someone if you needed help, but there was also the inability to remain invisible.

Did she miss Chicago? Well, yes and no. She missed her favorite café, but she'd had to seriously adjust her caffeine intake according to the guidelines for a pregnant woman. And the upscale dining? Yes, she missed that, too, though she'd heard The Oak Table was comparable to The Oak Bench. Interesting that they shared almost identical names. She'd wanted to give the restaurant a try but Mr. I'm-a-Player had ruined that idea when she spotted him cozying up at the restaurant bar with a gorgeous brunette. Maybe she'd try again tomorrow and she'd ask Meredith to accompany her since she was the one who'd recommended the place.

*Trust me*, she'd said. *The owner knows what he's doing. The Oak Bench has nothing on him.* The smile said there was more to those words but she'd just shrugged and said, *You'll see, give it time. And speaking of giving something time, don't be so hard on Ethan. I give him a lot of credit for packing up and following you here. I doubt he's ever done anything like that before, especially in regard to a woman.*

*So, what are you saying? I should throw my arms around him and ask him to marry me?*

*No, but I think you need to give him a chance...see where things go. I'm not saying you'll end up together or anything like that, but you can't deny the mutual attraction. I've seen it but you are stone-cold shutting the man down. Don't you think he's unsure of everything and how to progress with the baby? He has a right to be included and he wants to be. Do you have any idea how rare that is and how lucky you are? Even if nothing develops between you, he wants to be involved in the child's life. Give him a chance to do that. Don't be one of those women who tries to control every situation, including the baby she's carrying. It's not right for you or for the child.*

Meredith found the good in everyone and trusted that most people would do what they said they'd do. Vanessa didn't possess that innate ability to trust first, ask questions later. If Ethan Nance were involved in the baby's life, then what? It was a huge ask and it would leave Vanessa vulnerable. She'd been on her own for so long that she didn't want to depend on another person for help, especially with a baby. Vanessa pondered the question, tormented herself with the possibilities. What was right, what was fair, what was unfair. On and on it went until clarity came early one morning in the dining room of the bed-and-breakfast as she ate a bowl of oatmeal with blueberries and listened to Jennifer Merrick.

"I've been thinking about your situation. It's a difficult one and for that, I'm sorry." She clutched her coffee mug between her hands, said in a voice laced with pain. "I'd like to share something with you that I haven't told many people, but it might help you."

Jennifer told her the story of the husband she'd chosen over her own family, the one who promised to love her forever, care for her and about her...until she became pregnant. "He didn't want the baby; told me it wasn't part of the plan. *His* plan, I guess." Her eyes grew bright, shimmered with tears. "He wanted me to get rid of it, as if I would ever do that. Hope is my true joy. I divorced the man and he's never once attempted to see her, doesn't even know if he had a son or a daughter. Hope might have his DNA, but he is *not* her father." A tear slipped down her cheek, followed by another.

"I am so sorry."

"It took years for me to trust a man again, but I finally took the chance. He's the reason I was able to repair my relationship with my mother and forgive myself for the horrible choices I made. My father died before I could make things right with him. I spent years blaming my parents for my problems and refused to accept responsibility for my part in any of it. When I finally had the courage to open up to someone, that man helped me see that I couldn't change what happened, and I'd have to accept that if I were ever going to have a chance for peace or happiness. Realizing that was very freeing. Keep that in mind when you're making your decisions regarding Ethan Nance because believe it or not, your child *will* be affected." Pause and a sniff. "Hope is a true gift to me, but so is Oliver Donovan and I would never have believed that possible."

Meredith had mentioned Jennifer and Oliver, said that while there may or may not ever be wedding vows, the couple shared a true love story filled with second chances. "I think we share a similar story." Vanessa fought the tightness in her throat, pushed out the words that needed spoken. "Wrong choice in men, fracture in our relationship with our parents, pregnancy…"

Jennifer nodded. "But maybe the difference between our stories is that your baby's father *wants* to be a father and maybe he wants more…maybe he wants you."

∽

ETHAN CLEARED HIS THROAT, shifted his gaze to Vanessa. "Would you like me to wait outside?" Of course, she wanted him to leave the exam room while she changed, and he guessed if she had a choice, she'd ask him to keep walking...right out of her life.

Vanessa clutched the hospital gown against her belly, darted a glance at him. Hesitated. "You can stay."

"Are you sure?"

A nod, followed by a prim "Can you just turn around?"

"Of course." He faced the pregnancy chart, wished he hadn't. No way to unthink those visuals. Way too much information staring back at him. Ethan blinked, switched out visions of female reproductive organs with blankets of snow. They'd gotten dumped on last night: five inches of the white stuff that started just after midnight. Much of it had already been shoveled, plowed, and piled up to make sidewalks and roads navigable. He'd woken to the sound of a pickup truck with a plow attached clearing his driveway. No idea who'd done it, but Ethan figured Tate Alexander had a hand in it. Guess that was small-town hospitality in action, and he couldn't say he minded it.

"You can turn around now. What do you think? Model worthy, isn't it?"

Ethan pushed aside thoughts of snow and small towns and faced Vanessa. He would have sworn no one could look good, much less beautiful, in a blue-and-white print hospital gown, but this woman did. The pale blue side barrette she wore matched the blue in the hospital gown, enhanced the hazel of her eyes, drew the pink from her cheeks. But it was the vulnerability that surrounded her as she sat on the edge of the exam table in a hospital issue gown and floral socks that made her real...and beautiful. "I think it suits you." He tried to erase the emotion from his voice, failed. Oh, what the hell. "But then you don't need designer labels to be beautiful." More emotion. "You accomplish that all by yourself."

She stared. Opened her mouth, closed it.

"That didn't come out right." Talk about making an idiotic statement. Didn't matter if he thought it were true or not, point was he should have kept quiet. Ethan cleared his throat, stumbled to rephrase the comment. "What I meant to say was that you're beautiful without the high-end wardrobe."

Vanessa frowned. "You mean naked?"

"No. No!" What was happening to his brain? "That is not what I meant."

"Hmm."

He dragged a hand through his hair, searched for a scrap of intellect left in the gray matter some referred to as a brain. "I was speaking of your beauty on a more ethereal level."

"Oh. Thank you."

"You're welcome." Ethan clamped his mouth shut and did not say another word until the doctor came in the room and introduced herself. Dr. Dina Sarino. She reminded Ethan of a yoga instructor he'd once had: mid-50's, petite, salt-and-pepper hair, bright blue eyes. The information he'd gathered online along with the recommendation from the Donovans made him comfortable she was a reasonable choice. He would have preferred to do his own vetting, but he wasn't the only party involved in this decision. Hadn't Daniel told him compromise was key to any "relationship"? Yes, he was certain his pain-in-the-butt best friend had said exactly that. *What constituted a relationship anyway?*

"I have some questions and then we'll do the exam."

Competent, knowledgeable, compassionate, those were traits Ethan planned to look for as the doctor conducted the prenatal visit. But he also wanted to take notes because this first visit contained a lot of information. He pulled out a notepad, began writing as the doctor spoke. There was so much to comprehend. Had she said first trimester or second? Ethan scribbled, tried to keep up. What the heck had he just written?

"Dad?"

Ethan continued writing, his penmanship once again diminishing to a scribble. *Testing...glucose levels…*

"*Ethan.*"

"What?" He looked up, spotted Vanessa's pinched brows. "What's wrong?" He darted a glance at the doctor. "Is something wrong? She… Is it the baby?"

The gentle smile preceded Dr. Sarino's words. "You're going to have to get used to being called Dad. It's not uncommon to think a person is talking to someone else the first time you hear it, but you're the dad, Ethan." Compassion spread over her face, landed in her words. "Why don't you pause the note taking and if you want to know everything that's happening here, I'm fine with you recording this appointment, as long as Vanessa approves."

Ethan nodded, closed his notebook, and pulled out his phone. "That would make it much easier. Besides, I can barely read what I wrote and I think I'm missing too much." He glanced at Vanessa. "Would you be okay if I taped this appointment?"

"If it will make you relax, then yes." A hint of a smile played about her lips. "Go ahead and start taping. But no video!"

That made him smile. "No video. And thank you." There was no sense pretending he wasn't nervous, unsettled, and so far out of his element he might as well be the one on the exam table. The doctor waited for him to begin recording and continued the appointment. It was much easier to let the phone app do the work, so Ethan could actually concentrate on what she said. Ultrasounds...blood work...fetal heartbeat... There was so much information and so much testing. How did women have babies and make it to delivery without falling apart? He considered

himself and Vanessa reasonable people with above-average intelligence, and yet listening to the doctor as she laid out visits, tests,
and expectations made him just short of queasy.

"Are there any questions?"

*Yes, how are we ever going to get through this pregnancy?*
That's what he wanted to ask with a follow-up: *And what
happens when we get the baby home? What then? How are we
supposed to know what to do?*

Vanessa shook her head, waited for Ethan to comment. She
must have known he would have at least one question and maybe
that's why she didn't ask any of her own. Where should he start?
There were too many questions and not all of them had answers.
The kid hadn't even been born and Ethan was already covered
knee-deep with fear he couldn't protect the child. *Breathe.* One
breath at a time, that's how they would do it. "I'd like to listen to
the tape first and then I'll formulate questions if that's okay?" Dr.
Sarino was the expert, she'd guide them, and they'd have to trust
her. It was the only way they were going to make it through this
—trust—in the doctor and in each other.

"Absolutely. Take your time and reach out when you're
ready. I'm not worried about you two." Her voice softened. "I
think you'll both do just fine."

"Thank you." This from Vanessa whose hazel eyes glistened.

"I'd like to do an exam, just to check things out."

Ethan moved to the head of the exam table, clasped Vanessa's hand and held her gaze. He'd read there would be an exam
and wondered if she'd ask him to leave, but he didn't want to
leave. She squeezed his hand, held tight. Maybe she didn't want
him to leave either… Maybe she needed him here as much as he
wanted to be here.

They'd figure this parenting thing out together—side-by-
side. He'd never pictured himself in this situation, a father-to-be
who knew more about his cleaning lady than the woman carrying

his child. That was not okay and it was going to change. When the doctor finished her exam, she congratulated them once again, told them she looked forward to their next visit, when they would hear the heartbeat. Something shifted deep in Ethan's soul. He leaned over, helped Vanessa sit up, gathered her clothes, and faced the cream-colored wall and the chart with the pregnant woman's body parts. As he waited for her to dress, he vowed he would work hard to be a good dad and partner. But what kind of partner did he want to be? And what kind of partner did *she* want him to be? Friend, life partner, all of the above? He didn't know but he intended to find out.

## 12

The Oak Table really could take a place in Chicago alongside other upscale restaurants. Meredith had been right about that. She'd invited Vanessa for dinner the evening after the prenatal visit because, as she insisted a face-to-face retelling of the appointment was different than a phone conversation. What Meredith had not told Vanessa was that she would be interjecting her own thoughts and interpretation of the retelling.

"He's got a thing for you. It's so obvious."

Nothing was obvious with Ethan Nance. Yes, he'd been kind yesterday and there'd definitely been compassion. It would be untrue to pretend she didn't appreciate it. And when the appointment was over, she half expected him to invite her somewhere so they could share thoughts on how things went. She would have gone, too, but he hadn't extended the invitation. Instead, he'd seen her to her car, opened the door and thanked her for letting him be involved. One quick nod and a smile and he headed to his luxury sedan and drove away.

Just like that. There'd been no follow-up phone calls, no texts or emails in twenty-four hours.

"Vanessa, are you ignoring me?" Meredith sipped her margarita, blue eyes curious.

"No, not at all. I don't think there's much to say other than he plans to take an active part with the baby." The truth slipped out. "I'm beginning to realize what a monumental responsibility being a parent will be. I want to be a good mother, not one of those let-me-be-your-friend types who refuses to set ground rules and boundaries because they think the child won't love them."

The nod and soft "I agree" said Meredith understood.

"And I don't want to be an absent parent either. You know, leave the house before the child wakes up and come home at the tail-end of the bedtime story." She hadn't known what she wanted or how her life would look with a child, but once she changed into the hospital gown and Dr. Sarino began talking about the trimesters and the baby's development, that's when Vanessa knew spreadsheets and marketing plans would no longer be the center of her existence. They wouldn't be what she thought about late at night or woke up to in the morning. As the doctor checked her, Vanessa's world shifted, and the baby landed right in the middle of it. The only potential problem was that Ethan Nance, the man who'd held her hand with such caring and compassion, was part of this new world. "I've accepted the fact that his desire to be part of the baby's life means we'll have to learn to co-exist. I'm actually beginning to realize he could add value to the parenting aspect."

"Could add value?" Laughter spilled from Meredith. "Don't let him hear you say that like he's some sort of commodity." Another laugh. "Ethan would not appreciate that."

"Why not? The man prefers facts and numbers over emotion. I would think he'd understand exactly what I'm saying."

"Oh, he would and that's my point. Ethan would understand and he wouldn't like it." She shook her dark head, settled back in the booth. "You are so brilliant and yet sometimes you are so clueless. Why do you think he followed you to Reunion Gap, left his penthouse and his Ferrari and his upscale restaurants—" she waved a hand around The Oak Table "—though this is definitely Chicago-worthy?"

"He wants to be a part of the baby's life, which includes the prenatal exams, ultrasounds, birthing classes..."

"Baby shopping!" Meredith's eyes sparkled. "Can you picture Ethan in a baby store? I bet he'll agonize over the baby monitors."

"Agonize? I think he'll research the brands, read *all* of the reviews, and conduct his own studies. Do not be surprised if he purchases several models and tests them out himself." Vanessa's lips twitched as she pictured him testing each product and documenting his findings.

"Or, he could just ask people who actually use them, like Rogan and Elizabeth and Luke and Helena."

"Yes, he could, but he's the type of person who wants to draw his own conclusions, not that he wouldn't appreciate the input from trusted sources." That was actually a very good quality he possessed and Vanessa was much the same. Interesting that she "knew" that about him. Ethan Nance had been the one man who'd intrigued and challenged her and she'd looked forward to the conversations they'd had prior to the trip to Reunion Gap. It would be untrue to say she hadn't been curious and looking forward to meeting him in person. And that had presented a huge problem, because standing close enough to inhale the man's cologne while he spoke in that mesmerizing voice? Not good. And the laugh that made her insides heat up? Very bad. But those dark eyes and the lips? Irresistible. She might have denied the attraction and the desire from the instant he introduced himself, but who was she kidding? They were destined to spend the night together and that was one truth she couldn't ignore.

But why?

"So, do you really think the only reason he's camping out in Reunion Gap is because he doesn't want to miss the baby appointments? Chicago is a plane ride away and Logan's Creek, where he spends most of his time is a few hours' car ride." Meredith eyed her over her margarita glass. "He could pencil you in like I'm guessing he does every other part of his life. Unless—" her voice dipped, turned soft "—he hasn't figured you out or what to do about that. I think the two of you are going to discover you have a lot more in common than a baby. By the way, have you seen his place yet?"

Something in her expression made Vanessa wonder if Meredith possessed privileged information on the subject. "No, why?" She had wondered about the rental on the outskirts of town and how the updating was coming along. How did a man used to high-end chic adjust to a house that according to Meredith still didn't have a working dishwasher or garbage disposal? Yes, she'd been very curious about that one, but no doubt given enough time, he'd have them both installed. Still, it sounded like a huge shift from the man's normal lifestyle. Maybe being in Reunion Gap would bring out a more "relaxed" side of him. Yesterday was the first time she'd seen him without a suit jacket and tie. That was not 100 percent true—she had seen him without a jacket, tie, pants… She pushed that hot night away where she'd seen him without *any* clothes and concentrated on her friend. "You think I should swing by, bring him a basket of granola bars and water?"

A shrug, a tiny smile. "I'd switch out the granola for some-thing chocolate. Ethan loves anything chocolate, and I'll bet he'd appreciate the water, but... Remember when you used to tell me that a person had to experience a situation to truly appreciate it? It usually had to do with me drawing the wrong conclusions based on my past experiences. Well..."

"Well, what?"

"Ethan's a good guy. Daniel shared with me how he's helped him through a lot and I'm not just talking about business. If he hadn't sent the clip of Daniel telling the whole world who he was and how he named a collection after me, who knows how long it might've taken for us to realize we belonged together." She toyed with her wedding band, let the emotion spill. "I think buried somewhere beneath the cultured voice and fancy clothes is a sweet soul who wants to believe in love and ever after, even if he refuses to say the words."

Why would Meredith believe *that?* "I think the fact that you're head-over-heels for your husband has colored your view-point on the subject. Haven't you noticed couples in love tend to do that? They want everyone they meet to get paired off, fall in love, get married..." Look at how many couples she'd met the first time she visited Reunion Gap? Rogan and Elizabeth Donovan, Luke and Helena Donovan, Tate and Charlotte Alexander, Oliver Donovan and Jennifer Merrick.

Bright smiles, shared glances, fairytale notions. Ethan had joked about it but there'd been a twinge of something deep inside her that said maybe that wouldn't be so bad if a person could trust another person… If there was a partner... If... Meredith's next words sliced through her thoughts.

"This town and the people in it have a way of helping folks see what's important in life. I'm not just talking about romance and a partner, but finding joy, finding a path and a purpose that mean something. I'm so happy you'll be here for Christmas because it's a magical time. You'll see. Maybe something *magical* will happen between you and Ethan. Who knows?"

Meredith always believed the best in everyone. Vanessa didn't know if that was a good quality or a not-so-good quality. You could certainly get blindsided by that belief, but you could also find a lot of joy and Meredith had definitely found her joy.

On the other hand, trusting *no one* and questioning *everything* made for a lot of empty nights filled with the wrong person or no person... Disastrous relationships… Lots of doubt. Meredith might believe that Vanessa and Ethan had a chance together, but did she really think a man like Ethan Nance would ever open up and share his life? Maybe he was more interested in spending "moments" with beautiful women like the one she'd seen him with the other night. "I didn't plan to say anything but Ethan's not exactly a one-woman type of person, in case you haven't figured that out."

Meredith raised a brow, frowned. "That's the old Ethan you're talking about, not this one. Daniel said he's seen the change and Ethan might not have realized it yet, but he's different. Edgier, maybe confused... And that is *not* Ethan Nance. Daniel thinks you're responsible for that behavior."

"Tell him a baby on the way might be responsible for the edginess *and* the confusion."

"That is not what Daniel's talking about. He noticed the change before Ethan knew you were pregnant. I'm just saying he might be smitten and he's going to fight it just like Daniel did. And just like Daniel, he's going to lose."

Vanessa clutched her water glass, sucked in a breath. "I saw him here with someone the other night. A beautiful woman and he definitely looked more than a little interested."

"Really? I find that hard to believe."

Of course, Meredith would say that. "It's because you only want to believe in the goodness in people, but..."

"Hmm. I know most of the people in this town or I know of them. Small towns are that way. You can be gone forever and once you return it only takes a little bit before you know who's who, who's with whom, and everything in between. So, what's this woman look like? Tall, short, full-figured, thin? Blonde, brunette? Give me the details and I'll ferret her out and get the truth." Meredith set her margarita on the table, leaned forward. "Spit it out. Tell me everything you know."

"It doesn't matter who it is. Really, it's fine. The man doesn't owe me anything." But the genuine compassion and the way he'd looked at her yesterday during the prenatal visit made her wonder if he might be interested in more than the baby.

"Just tell me, okay?"

Meredith was not going to stop until Vanessa provided information. "Fine. She was tall or appeared to be. Hard to tell since she was sitting at the bar. I did notice long legs. No doubt he noticed them, too. And she was a brunette; long hair, fell to the mid-back, wavy." She really did not want to do this. "But tomorrow it could be a redhead and a blonde the day after that. The man's a player and he's not interested in being a one-woman man." Vanessa sipped her water so she didn't spill out anything else like, *I've thought about it, but even if I were interested, he's a bad investment.*

"So, she was a tall brunette with long hair. What else do you have?" Meredith's voice shifted a few decibels higher as she compiled information. "You mentioned they were sitting at the bar. If they'd been in a booth, then it might have been a planned meeting. This was more of an incidental encounter."

"Oh, you mean a pickup." And maybe that "incidental encounter" ended in his Cape Cod on the outskirts of town, and maybe that pickup didn't leave his bed before morning.

"What night was he here? If you give me the details I'll ask my friend Nicki. Her husband owns this place."

"Nicki from the wedding? The one who was your matron of honor?" Vanessa remembered her, but she didn't recall meeting the husband. In fact, hadn't someone said he wasn't there? Something about a sick child and babysitting duty.

A quick nod and a splash of red across her cheeks. "Yes, that's Nicki."

"So, why not just ask the husband about the woman? Not that I want you to do anything, but I've always found cutting out extraneous data gets more reliable answers. Too much information gets distorted and lost in translation."

"Wow, now you sound like Ethan. Extraneous data?" The red seeped from her cheeks to the rest of her face. "I can't ask Nicki's husband."

"Because?" Why had she started to squirm?

"I'm not his favorite person." She rubbed her temples, cleared her throat. "I messed up pretty bad by jumping to conclusions. I was only trying to help, but I almost cost them their marriage. I thought he was cheating with his old girlfriend and…" Her voice trailed off, her eyes filled with tears. "I don't think he'll ever forgive me for what I did but I am not going to stop trying to earn that forgiveness. At least Nicki has forgiven me, but other than the niceties of 'how are you' and 'good to see you again,' I can't ask anything more of him. I'm just grateful he hasn't banned me from this place."

So, Meredith had been poking around in other people's business, made incorrect assumptions, and created a huge problem. "It's really not a big deal. I don't need you to snoop around and find answers. If I really wanted to know, I'd ask Ethan myself." *That* was so not true and the look on Meredith's face said she knew it.

"Okay then, but if you change your mind, I can ask Nicki. How about we order? I love the salmon but everything is good here. Plus, you have to save room for dessert. There's a triple chocolate lava cake that explodes the senses in a very good way."

And just like that, talk of a potential relationship with Ethan Nance fizzled. Meredith was correct about the food selection. Vanessa chose the salmon, and the smashed cauliflower with asparagus proved truly delicious. Of course, she was not going to turn down the opportunity for chocolate. The waitress had just delivered a triple chocolate lava cake with a dollop of ice cream and two spoons when the mystery brunette walked into the restaurant and slid onto a barstool. "Meredith? *That's her.*" Dark hair, perfect figure, long legs. Meredith had been poised to drop a spoonful of lava cake and ice cream in her mouth, when she paused, turned around.

"Are you talking about the woman in the lavender turtleneck and black slacks?"

"Right. How much do you want to bet Ethan Nance will show up?"

Meredith turned back around, plopped the lava-cake-ice cream mixture into her mouth, chewed. The sigh came next followed by the smile. "So delicious." She spooned another piece of lava cake, sighed again. "As to the woman in the lavender turtleneck... How about if you're wrong you have to visit Ethan...at his house...and bring him something chocolate?"

Why would she make a comment like that? "Sure, fine, I'll do it, but you just wait. He's going to show up, I'll bet my computer on it."

"Don't bet what you can't afford to lose." Meredith's voice slipped into a singsong tone. "You're going to lose this one, wait and see."

Vanessa homed in on the mystery woman, watched as a handsome dark-haired man emerged from the kitchen, leaned over, and gave her a peck on the cheek. "What the heck?"

Meredith glanced over her shoulder. "So, that's Nicki's husband, Jameson. He couldn't make the wedding." Pause and a doubtful "Nicki said the babysitter cancelled last minute and one of the kids was sick, but I know the babysitter is Jameson's mother or one of his sisters. That woman at the bar? That's his sister and she's definitely *not* on the hunt. Last I heard she was on the verge of an engagement offer. So..."

"So, she and Ethan aren't interested in each other?" Vanessa sipped in tiny breaths of air, tried to make sense of it all.

"Nope." Meredith pointed her spoon at Vanessa. "Like I told you, that man's only interested in one person and that person is you." She continued to attack the lava cake. "So, when are you going to visit Ethan? And don't forget the chocolate—he likes dark."

## 13

Ethan should have known it was only a matter of time before Daniel figured out he knew the difference between a miter saw and a table saw and how to use both. It wasn't that Ethan never planned to tell his best friend; it was more that he didn't want the questions that would accompany the revelation. *What do you mean you know how to use a router and a planer? Where would you have learned that? And why?* And then the bigger question, the one that would land square between them, threaten their friendship. *Why wouldn't you tell me? All this time... Why wouldn't you just tell me the truth?*

If he had his choice, Ethan would have planned the disclosure down to the last detail. And maybe he would have even tried for a bit of humor such as placing all of the tools he'd been using side-by-side, naming them and their uses, and offering a demonstration. But he had no time for any of it because Daniel landed on his doorstep two days after the prenatal visit. Ethan had been diligent about locking the doors because in a small town like Reunion Gap, people might just take it upon themselves to knock and then walk in with a quick *Hello, anybody there?* But apparently, he hadn't been as diligent as he thought. He'd been carrying a piece of trim and had gotten involved fitting it into a tight space when he heard Daniel's voice.

"Hey, anybody there?"

*Damn, so much for locking the door.* Ethan eyeballed the fitting, marked the board. There was no good way to handle this so he might as well deal with it straight up. "In here."

"Ethan? Hey buddy, what are you doing?" Footsteps...and then "Isn't there too much sawdust in this... What the hell?"

"Can you grab that level on the table?" Ethan glanced at Daniel. "I'm trying to get this piece of casing to fit between the window and the cupboard and I'm having a tough time."

Daniel didn't move. He stared, frowned. "What the hell are you doing?"

"The level?"

Daniel grabbed it, placed it on the window. "You're square. Nail the damn thing in and start talking."

Ethan pounded in three nails and faced his best friend. "I know how to use a router and a planer. I prefer to install trim with a nail gun, but a hammer will do in a pinch." The scowl said Daniel wasn't interested in a router or a planer. "Just because I know how to use these tools doesn't mean I want to or didn't want to until I came here." Ethan leaned against the kitchen counter, crossed his arms over his chest, wished he were wearing a suit and tie—his armor and camouflage—instead of faded jeans and an old sweatshirt. "I learned out of necessity. My father took off when I was just a kid. My mother wanted to make sure I didn't need anything, even if we couldn't afford it. She never understood the concept of money in, money out, which is no doubt why I'm obsessed with spreadsheets and calculations. I was fifteen when I learned we were near bankruptcy. Yeah, that's when I gained firsthand knowledge of debt collectors, late charges, utility shut-offs, and reinstatement fees. Before that, I never thought about money or how much we did or didn't have. Why would I when she was buying me designer jeans, sending me to summer camps, making sure I had the newest electronic gadgets? But once I found out how bad it was, I knew I had to help, so I found a job with a handyman."

Ethan dragged a hand through his hair, fought the memories of the delinquent bills and shut-off notices. "I started working after school to earn money and pay down debt. I tried to explain to my mother how I didn't need the latest and greatest of everything and how a credit score is as valuable as a college education." He let out a laugh, shook his head. "I still don't think she agrees. It became a battle and I compromised. I worked to pay down her debt and she never stopped trying to tell me I deserved everything I wanted—even when I didn't. So yeah, am I a control freak who plans every second to avoid unintended consequences? Sure, or at least I had been."

Daniel's shoulders relaxed, the dark expression lightened, replaced with what looked an awful lot like sympathy. "I'm sorry it was so rough for you."

"Do *not* feel sorry for me. I hate that. I am not anyone's cause. Got it?"

A nod, a narrowed gaze followed by "You're my best friend. I should have known this about you." Pause and a cautious "If there's any other critical information you're withholding, now would be the time to tell me if you value our friendship." The scowl returned. "All of it, not just the abridged version."

"Why don't you sit down? This could take a while." And then he shared the story of Darcy Pennington, the only woman he'd ever loved, the one he planned to share his life with...the one he watched die. The telling of that tragic story made Ethan feel less isolated and he hadn't felt that way in a long time. He even shared the part about how he still visited Darcy's mother several times a year, had bought her a home that she filled with memories of her daughter, and listened when she sometimes acted as though Darcy were merely away, and not gone forever.

"I can't risk that kind of loss again." Ethan's voice turned hoarse, cracked. "I just can't, no matter who it is." That was his way of explaining why he wouldn't and *couldn't* get involved with anyone in a serious relationship—no matter the circumstances.

Daniel pinned him with that blue stare. "You mean Vanessa."

It wasn't even a question. The man knew exactly who he meant. Ethan let out a loud sigh. "Doesn't matter who it is. I can't do it."

"I'm not sure you have a choice. You see, the heart does what it wants, even when the brain tries to stop it. Take it from a guy who's lived it."

He meant the debacle with Meredith. Ethan had tried to warn him to go slow, don't get involved with her until he'd completed the "job" he'd been sent to do, which involved pretending to be someone else. Of course, the guy didn't listen. Apparently, that's what he meant about the heart not listening to the brain. Well, that heart hadn't listened to Ethan either and the fallout was disastrous and almost cost Daniel the woman he loved. But this situation wasn't the same. "I appreciate the concern and the recommendations, but I just have to be more careful when I'm around her."

"Okay." Daniel leaned back in the kitchen chair, studied him. "How do you plan to do that? Do you mean you'll stick to a script when you see her? Practice the words and the tone? Avoid eye contact? Hell, avoid looking at her—period?"

Ethan sighed. "Don't be ridiculous. I'm not a teenager. I know how to handle myself."

That comment made Daniel laugh. "No one will argue that,

especially me. I've been witness to dozens of broken hearts, usually from women you've forgotten before dinner's over. But —" those blue eyes homed in on him as though he could see inside Ethan's brain to the confusion and uncertainty "—not Vanessa. She's different and we all know it. Meredith has been tracking this 'destined relationship' as she calls it from the second you sent Vanessa the video clip of me at the Chicago unveiling. That's when she noticed Vanessa's obsession with her phone and email, and according to Meredith, there was real laughter coming from that office—usually when the two of you were having a conversation."

Ethan was not going to get pulled into a discussion on feelings and relationships and how destiny could guide a couple to forever and whatever. "Look, I explained my past so you'd understand, not so you could counsel me on my future."

Daniel studied him a few seconds too long before he pushed back his chair and nodded. "Got it. You're not going to get involved with Vanessa Rodelle on a personal basis other than the baby and the fact that you've already been involved." His lips twitched and he nodded again. "Sure, makes perfect sense to me."

"Shut up."

"Good luck with that plan. We've been best friends and business partners a long time, but this is by far the most incoherent and doomed-to-fail plan I've ever heard from you. But feel free to execute."

"Everybody doesn't need a soulmate." Too dangerous, too debilitating, too risky.

Daniel sliced him with a look and this time when he spoke there was an edge to his voice. "They don't, but once they find that person, they sure as hell don't want to let her go—no matter what they have to do to keep her."

Ethan stood, pushed in his chair. He was done with this conversation. "Thanks for stopping by and would you not tell anyone I'm doing work on this house?"

"Sure, I can do that."

"Including your wife?" Once Meredith found out, how long would it take before she told Vanessa? The questions would follow. *Where did you learn how to use a drill and work a miter saw? Why didn't you ever mention it?* And then the big one; *Why did you pretend you had no idea how to even hold a tool, much less what to do with it?* He did not want to deal with the questions and the insinuations that implied he'd been keeping secrets and those secrets could tarnish the stellar reputation he'd built for himself.

"Meredith and I don't keep secrets from each other." Daniel cleared his throat, added, "Not anymore."

"Right. Well then..." Once she learned about this, there was no keeping that woman quiet. She'd read all sorts of things into it instead of the truth; what he did and didn't do was no one's business. But with a person like Meredith Alexander Reese, everyone's business was her business, especially when she thought she could help them.

"How about I slow-walk the information to my wife?" Daniel rubbed his jaw, considered the possibility. "I think I could buy you two days, max. That will give you time to figure out what you're going to tell everyone who hears about it...including Vanessa."

"Sure, I'll work on my story." Ethan dragged a hand through his hair, didn't care that he'd probably left chunks standing up. "Why can't Meredith be more like her brother? Tate's known about this for days and even connected me to builder supply places. The guy's been great and his wife hasn't been nosing around."

"Maybe he didn't tell her."

"I'm pretty sure he did."

Daniel shrugged as if acknowledging his wife's busybody tendencies. "I can buy you forty-eight hours, so start working on your story."

## 14

Vanessa had never considered herself a creative person, but the idea for an additional headband line came to her when she was eating breakfast in Jennifer Merrick's dining room. The bed-and-breakfast had the most beautiful lace tablecloth with such intricate work and she'd been intrigued by it. She'd traced the pattern with a finger, studied it, visualized a headband made of lace on a baby girl. What would that look like? Headbands were certainly a thing, or at least several of the baby magazines she'd been reading showed baby girls wearing them. Were those just for the baby models or did "real" babies wear them?

What would it look like if a mother and child wore coordinating headbands? Wouldn't that make a great photo opportunity? As Vanessa considered this, she thought of the fabric possibilities. Some might contain lace, while others would be softer fabrics with patterns ranging from bold and bright to pastel or cream. The design could vary from basic to elaborate, with flowers and tiny ribbons attached. The ideas and the possibilities stayed with her for the next few days until she finally put thought to action.

Vanessa and Meredith were working in Camille Alexander's dining room, which served as the perfect makeshift office. Camille was in Austria with her lawyer beau and had offered up the elaborate residence for the next several weeks. Who wouldn't take advantage of such a generous offer? She'd also extended an invitation for Vanessa to stay there, but that had felt like too huge an imposition. True, the place was empty aside from a handful of staff, but it was still someone's home—and it was massive and austere. Vanessa preferred the coziness of the bed-and-breakfast and she enjoyed Jennifer Merrick's company. The woman was kind, compassionate, a good listener, and she didn't judge.

"So, what's the big reveal you want to share?" Meredith had been sketching a headband for next year's "spring festival" collection, which would focus on four main colors: orange, green, pink, and gray.

"What do you think about coordinating mother and daughter headbands?" Vanessa placed her hands on the linen tablecloth, leaned toward her friend. "We could start with babies, continue to toddlers, and beyond, all the way up to teenagers if we wanted. Imagine Christmas-themed coordinated headbands. I think they'd work well in holiday photos and how about seasonal ones? There's a lot you can do with that concept." More ideas swirled through her head. "Well, what do you think?"

Meredith's face lit up, her voice a gush of excitement. "I love it! Oh, Vanessa, your creativity's surging. I'll bet it's because of the baby."

"What?"

"The baby. I'll bet the pregnancy is getting everything pumping and channeling areas you didn't know existed. Like the creativity you've always said you didn't have." Meredith clasped her hand, squeezed. "So go with it. I love, love, love it!" And then "Have you considered the market for this? It could be huge."

Yes, she had considered the market, but oddly that hadn't been the primary focus and for someone who was numbers-driven, this was stunning. "I *have* thought about it, but not to the degree I usually do. I can work up a few ideas and projections, do a market analysis… And maybe you can sketch some ideas? Come up with a few patterns you think could work?"

"Me?" Meredith squeezed her hand again. "I think this should be all you."

"I'm not the creative focus here. I don't… It was just an idea, but I wouldn't know what to do with it as far as making it a reality."

"How can you say that? You basically came up with an idea that I hadn't considered, and you told me how we could use it. More importantly, *you're* the one who thought about designs and fabric. You absolutely have to take the lead on this one. Don't you see that when passion follows purpose, magic happens? Haven't I always told you that?"

Yes, Meredith had told her that, but she'd also told her a lot of things that Vanessa had tossed aside as Meredith being Meredith in an overzealous, much-too-spontaneous way. But maybe she wasn't so far off in this particular area because Vanessa *had* come up with ideas and created a few basic sketches and she couldn't stop thinking about what it all might look like, who would wear it, for what occasion. Maybe she *could* do it. "You really think so?"

"I don't just think so." Meredith grinned. "*I know so*. This is over-the-top exciting. I think we should start working on this asap. What do you think?"

"I guess?" This whole idea was so far out of Vanessa's scope that she found it hard to believe she'd be capable of doing it. Meredith was the creator. Meredith was the one who matched fabric with design and focused on the details. But maybe Vanessa *could* work on a project with her. Or maybe Meredith could work on this project with Vanessa as the lead. Yes, maybe...

"Creativity at work. I love it." Meredith's voice turned soft. "Maybe one day I'll have a surge of pregnancy creativity." The pink cheeks and gentle smile said *maybe one day soon.*

So, Daniel and Meredith wanted a baby. Vanessa waited for Meredith to say more but she didn't. Instead, she shifted the focus back to baby-mother coordinated headbands. "How about we grab some lunch at the Cherry Top Diner and toss around a few ideas? I'm dying for a turkey Reuben, smothered with Thousand Island dressing and a big slice of cherry pie. What do you think?"

Vanessa had never subscribed to a traditional lunch. In fact, she often skipped lunch or substituted it with a smoothie. But that was before the pregnancy and Ethan's report on what constituted healthy eating. *You can have a smoothie but it has to have greens and watch the sugars. Plus, you should eat whole foods. Remember, carbs are not the enemy, but you have to be smart about them. I've compiled a go-to list to help make the choices easier.* Vanessa pushed Ethan Nance's lecture away and said, "I was thinking about the wedding soup and who can resist coconut cream pie?" *Carbs are not the enemy, but you have to make smart choices.* "Or a double fudge brownie. Or both?"

"Yum and yum." Meredith grabbed her handbag and said, "I'll drive." They made their way to the three-story foyer and were out the door before Meredith shared a bit of news Vanessa hadn't expected. "So, I'm getting a little tired of working at my aunt's dining room table. Sure, the table's huge and nobody bothers us—" she opened her car door, slid inside "—but there are times when I feel the need for more of a business environment." Meredith laughed, headed down the long driveway. "Daniel must be rubbing off on me. We've been having long discussions on creativity and making the work fill the day as opposed to getting the work done. I tend to procrastinate, big surprise there, and he's called me on it a few times. I'm trying to be more aware of how I spend my day, a.k.a. time management."

"Time management?" Wow, who would have thought Daniel could get Meredith to consider what an effective versus an ineffective day looked like? Vanessa had tried and failed for months.

"Yup, how bizarre is that?"

"Quite." Almost unbelievable.

"Anyway, Tate's offered the use of one of his offices at the company. He's got a pretty swanky setup. All we have to do is say yes, but if you want to look at it first, we can do that, too. Whatever you want."

"I actually like working in a more relaxed environment but I do appreciate the offer. Maybe if we have to bring people in for meetings, we could borrow his conference room."

"Sure, he's offered and I know he'll be fine with it. Daniel's working with Tate on buying a piece of property with a barn that could be renovated into his workshop. I can't wait to be back here on a more permanent basis." She let out a wistful sigh. "Daniel's looking forward to it, too. And once we have kids..." Her voice drifted off as though she were imagining that day.

"I'm really happy for you, Meredith." Not everyone got a happily-ever-after, but at least this couple had, and they deserved it.

"Thank you." Her blue eyes turned bright, glistened with emotion. "If you stay here, there will be plenty of people to help out with the baby, and lots of support. But no matter where you go, I have a feeling Ethan will be there, too."

"It sure sounds like it." Was that a good thing? Would it be so bad to see him on a regular basis, maybe even every day? Talk to him about non-baby matters? Did she want that? Oh, who was she kidding? The truth was beginning to leach into her thoughts; she did want to spend more time with him, get to know him for reasons that had nothing to do with the baby, and denying it any longer would be a lie. Unfortunately, she was beginning to realize a lot more about what she wanted with Ethan Nance and therein lay problem number one, which segued into problem number two. She had no idea what to do about it.

Spending a few hours with Meredith at the Cherry Top Diner discussing possibilities for a coordinated mother-daughter head-band line, offering pattern and fabric options, even sketching out a few designs, made Vanessa excited about the business and the possibilities in ways she hadn't felt in a very long time. Had she *ever* been this excited about a project? Hard to say, because she'd always tried to temper her enthusiasm in order to mitigate potential pitfalls and the disappointments that might create less-than-stellar outcomes.

But this time felt different because she was not thinking about failure or minimizing the risk. No, she was only thinking about possibility and passion and planned to let her imagination and enthusiasm forge the path. Plus, she had Meredith as her personal cheerleader, encouraging and guiding her. It was this support that made Vanessa bold, made her believe she might just be creative, might have an opportunity to experience magic. And maybe that magic would extend to her personal life as well.

## 15

Vanessa hadn't been interested in Christmas in years, but this year was different. The shops along the main street were decorated with twinkle lights in the windows and wreaths on the doors. Wooden candy canes hung from the streetlamps, secured by red bows. The gigantic Christmas tree in the center of town had been trimmed with twinkle lights, garlands, and hundreds of what looked like hand-made ornaments: balls, stars, stockings, trees, angels, reindeer, and so much more. And on top of the tree rested a brilliant star!

Enchanting. Magnificent. Inspiring.

Was this year different because she could appreciate the simple beauty of the season without being smothered with blaring horns, exhaust fumes, and too many people? She could draw in full, clean breaths, witness snow-covered pine trees that were not part of a display window or department store setup. Maybe it was the spirit of the small town and its people: welcoming, friendly, eager to pull her in to the festivities of Reunion Gap that made her anxious for the holiday.

Or was it because of the baby? Many women vowed that pregnancy accounted for a shift in their mood, a sense of wonder and excitement, and a true gratitude for the gift of life. Vanessa understood this sentiment though six months ago she would have insisted such a feeling did not exist.

But it did.

And perhaps somewhere jumbled in the middle of it all were her feelings for Ethan Nance. Hopeful? Uncertain? Curious? She had no idea and yet after her conversation with Meredith yesterday, she realized it was time to stop avoiding the man and pay him a visit. What could be the downside of a visit? Vanessa clutched the container of triple-dark-chocolate cookies she'd bought from the bakery, the ones Meredith insisted anyone with a chocolate tooth like Ethan would devour. How had she missed the fact that he loved chocolate?

What else had she missed?

She cleared her throat, made her way up the walk toward the white Cape Cod with red shutters. Someone had shoveled the driveway this morning. Or had it been plowed? Vanessa couldn't tell the difference but then she bet neither could Ethan. The outside reminded her of a house one might see on a Christmas card with pine trees and snow covering the bushes; quaint and cozy. Those words did not describe Ethan Nance. He was a penthouse-custom-designer sort of guy: upscale, classic, very chic.

But this house? All it needed was a string of lights decorating the windows and a wreath with a red bow on the front door. She almost wished she'd asked Tate Alexander if he had any other rentals, but it wouldn't have been practical and she'd have missed out on time with Jennifer Merrick. Plus, the meals were a nice bonus since the woman cooked whatever whim struck Vanessa; mushroom barley soup, grilled chicken with roasted peppers, veggie burgers. And the desserts? She'd limited those to every other day, but on the "yes" days? Banana bread, sugar cookies, blueberry muffins. Oh, such sweetness.

Vanessa rang the doorbell of Ethan's rental, wondered if she should have called first to make sure she wasn't interrupting his workday. The man appeared as particular as she was about efficiency and focus in the workplace, and while a home setting could prove a bit distracting, no doubt he'd get as much or more done despite that. She could not say the same, but the setting had little to do with her "distraction." A baby on the way could make a person reconsider her priorities, and relocating to a small town where you could think and feel and stop the chatter in your head? Well, that made you reconsider your *life* and what it should look like and if you—

"Vanessa?"

"Ethan?" She eyed the T-shirt and faded jeans. "You look…"

He raised a brow. "Out of my element? Unrecognizable?" He stepped aside, let her enter. "Ridiculous?"

"No. No!" Was that paint splattered on his tennis shoes? Her gaze inched back to his face and the unsmiling lips, the stern expression. He hadn't wanted her to see him like this. "You look normal."

"Normal?" His expression shifted, relaxed, and a hint of a smile appeared. "Now that is a compliment I can use on a resume."

"I didn't mean it that way." She thrust the box of triple-dark-chocolate cookies at him, eager to change the awkward moment. "I brought you something. Meredith said you love dark chocolate."

"Meredith says a lot of things, not all accurate." Ethan took the box from her, slid open the tab and let out a long, satisfied sigh before removing a cookie. "But she's correct on this one. I am obsessed with anything chocolate, especially dark chocolate." He extended the box to her. "I even share on occasion."

Vanessa removed a cookie, bit into it, enjoyed the sweet rush of chocolate. Ethan eased a cookie from the box, devoured half of it in one bite, no attempt to pretend indifference with smaller bites. She liked this relaxed version of Ethan Nance. Not so uptight, in control, determined to be right. This one was more approachable, but that still begged the question: why was the man wearing jeans and a T-shirt, and not designer ones either? "Why are you dressed like you're ready to paint or fix something?"

He stuffed the rest of the cookie in his mouth and when he'd finished chewing, he gave her an answer she'd never expected. "Because I am?" He helped her out of her coat, folded it over his arm. "I stained the trim for the downstairs bedrooms last night and I plan to hang it later today."

Vanessa stared at him. "*You're* doing that?" She listened for sounds that would indicate someone else was in the house but all she heard were the lyrics to *Sweet Emotion* reaching her from another room.

Ethan placed the box of cookies on an entry table, hung her coat in the tiny closet by the front door. His back was to her when he answered, "Sure, why not? Even 'suits' can learn how to hammer a nail."

Had she offended him? That certainly hadn't been her intent but having the man admit he not only understood the meaning of manual labor but engaged in it? That was a shocker. "Of course, I didn't mean you couldn't." Pause and then "Only that you wouldn't."

The shrug and the smile said it was no big deal, but she didn't think that was true as she recalled the comment Meredith once made about him. *Ethan avoids Daniel's workshop, says he's allergic to sawdust.* Wouldn't whatever he'd been doing in this house create some sort of sawdust? And if so, then why—

"Come on, I'll give you a tour of the place and show you what I've done."

"Sure." So, they were going to pretend it was perfectly normal for him to stain trim and do whatever other work he'd been doing? "I do have a question for you. Where did the real Ethan Nance go and who is this impostor who's taken his place?"

Laughter spilled from him, a real laugh, not forced or contrived. "Did you ever think there's more than one side to a person? Just because you can't see every side doesn't mean they don't exist."

Now that sounded like the Ethan Nance she knew. "Or maybe he does a very good job of hiding the sides he doesn't want to reveal."

"Or someone hasn't been paying attention," he shot back "There's always the obvious story and then there's the *other* story, the one found in the space between the words, the one gleaned from careful observation."

"I'm very certain I would have noticed the spaces *and* the behavior that indicated you were this person." Vanessa pointed to his less-than-perfect hair, T-shirt, and jeans. "Very certain."

Ethan jabbed a finger at his chest. "This person? This person and the guy in the suit are the same one but I like to keep them separate. Or I did until I landed in this town. There's something about this place that makes you start wondering about a lot of things. Why is it so important to act like you've never been hungry or worn hand-me-down jeans...or been miserable?" His voice dipped, his expression softened. "A place like this gives you time to think and ask questions, and if the answers you find aren't ones you like, then you ask more questions, and at some point, you realize you have to stop hiding. I'm not saying *I'm* hiding, just that I have a persona I like to project."

Oh, but this side of Ethan was very attractive. Too attractive. Vanessa ignored the warning signs that said *Be careful. You could get hurt. Be careful.* "I wish I could say I had no idea what you're talking about, but I do."

"I figure since we'll eventually be spending more time

together, I can't keep wearing a suit every time I see you because that would be very uncomfortable, so…"

"So, if I hadn't stopped by today, at what point would you have shared the I-wear-jeans-and-I-can-laugh-at-myself Ethan Nance? Would it have been after the baby was born, or would you have introduced that person in small segments? One day no tie, then no suit jacket, then no…"

He cleared his throat, and the burn in those dark eyes told her he was thinking about the night they shared at the bed-and-breakfast where he'd removed a lot more than a suit jacket and tie.

"I'm not sure when I would have told you, but it would've been a while yet." He paused, reworked his last words. "That's not exactly true. I had a forty-eight-hour window."

"What? Why?"

He motioned her to follow him into the tiny kitchen where he set the cookies on the counter, turned to her. "Daniel found out about my hidden talents two days ago and it did not go well. He gave me the whole lecture on how you're not supposed to keep things from your best friend and friendship involves telling the whole truth, not just the parts you don't mind sharing. You get the picture." He rubbed the back of his neck, let out a long sigh. "And when I asked him to keep it from Meredith, he said they didn't keep secrets anymore. Yeah, I wanted to tell him he would've been a lot better off if he hadn't kept secrets from the start, but there was no sense going there. He gave me forty-eight hours to do what I needed to do, as in tell you, not tell you or whatever I planned to do, because he was going to share this with Meredith."

"Oh boy, and we all know where that would have gone." Meredith always meant well, but she couldn't quite stay out of other people's lives, especially when she believed getting involved would help someone. Yes, she'd gotten better, but she was still Meredith, still bent on matching people up, one good deed at the time. "I wonder if she suspected something about you because she asked if I'd been to your place yet and if not, why? Something in the way she said it made me curious about that comment."

Ethan shook his head. "This is Meredith we're talking about. She loves Daniel and she wants to save the world but sometimes…"

"Sometimes she gets involved where she shouldn't." Vanessa had witnessed many of those "sometimes" and the fallout from them.

Ethan rolled his eyes. "Exactly. Well, when she tells you all about how I know the difference between a slide rule and a ruler, you can play it anyway you like: shocked, disinterested, curious. You can even laugh."

"Why would I laugh? I wish I had a tiny bit of a tradesman's skillset. I can barely change a light bulb and have always been fascinated by people who can fix or create things." Oh, how she wanted to ask him how he'd learned about home repairs but she wouldn't. There was a reason he hadn't shared this part of himself and she would respect that. Maybe in time he'd tell her. Or she'd piece together the spaces between *his* words and add them to her *observations* to formulate an opinion that inched toward the truth. "Will you show me what you've done and how you ended up in this particular house?"

He hesitated a second as if considering what and how much to tell her. Then his shoulders relaxed and he began to speak. "When I asked Tate if he had anything available, he told me about this place, but said it wasn't move-in ready. I actually liked that because I figured why not see if I remembered how to use a drill and work a miter saw? It's been a lot of years since I hung trim or replaced a vanity but it all came back to me. It took a little longer than it should have and I had to read the instructions and watch a few how-to videos, but I finally got it. Tate said this place needs a new dishwasher and garbage disposal and I plan to install those, too."

"But...this is a rental. You're doing all of this because...?"

Ethan shrugged, said in a quiet voice. "Because it feels good and it feels right. Tate said he'll offset the rent with whatever work I do, but I told him to give the money to someone who needs it." His dark eyes turned bright, sparked. "Like a single mother who's struggling."

And just like that, Ethan Nance surprised her once again. Such a compassionate gesture from a man who did his best to hide these traits. Why did he feel the need to pretend he didn't care about other people? And what did he know about a single mother who was struggling, unless... Had his mother been that person? "That's very kind."

Another shrug, followed by a burst of color splashing his cheeks. "Thank you."

"Do you think Tate would consider selling this place?" It was small and quaint, and just right for a baby. Vanessa had no idea where she'd end up, but Reunion Gap was on her list of possibilities. If she stayed here, this house could be perfect for her and the baby.

"I don't know. I imagine he would if the situation were right." He eyed her, his tone casual. "I might even put a bid in on this place."

"Really?" She'd never pictured him in a house that wasn't loaded with glass, chrome, and lots of leather.

"Maybe. I always thought I'd split my time between Chicago and Logan's Creek, but...there's a lot that's undecided."

## 16

W hat did he mean when he said *there's a lot that's undecided?* Was he referring to her and the baby as part of the "undecided"? Curiosity forced Vanessa to prod a bit more. "So, you could see yourself living in Reunion Gap?"

"Provided the circumstances lent themselves to the possibility, then yes, I could. There's a quiet calm about this town that's very appealing." Pause and a smile. "And the people. I like them, too."

"I agree. I don't know if it's my lack of busyness or my desire to figure out what the rest of my life will look like…or if it's hormones. But for the first time in a lot of years, I'm excited." She sighed, said in a soft voice, "And I'm especially excited about Christmas this year. Is that silly?"

"Not at all." His gaze shot to her belly, darted back to her face. "There's a lot to be thankful for this year."

"Yes, there is." As they stood in the kitchen and talked, Vanessa didn't have to fight for words because they just fell out. Stress-free. Easy. Comfortable. In many ways it felt like that first night in Reunion Gap when they'd finally met in person and talked for hours. The attraction had been instant and strong, though she'd worked hard to deny it. But there was something about the man that drew her to him, made her want to get closer, made her want to—

"So, let me show you what I've been doing instead of analyzing data and building spreadsheets. I painted the kitchen cabinets, removed the baseboards, and door and window casings. I also replaced the light fixtures because it was too dark and dingy in here. The new flooring should be in soon and it will finish off this room."

They spent the next forty minutes moving from room to room where Ethan showed her the new bathroom vanity and sink he'd installed, the ceiling fans he'd recently hung, and the newly painted walls. When they reached the first bedroom in the back of the house, Vanessa took in the queen-size bed, plain dresser, and tiny closet. "Do not even tell me this is your room because no way would your clothes fit in that closet. I'll bet your shoes wouldn't even fit in there."

He laughed. "True, but there's another bedroom next to this one with an equal size closet. If that's not enough, I'll hijack the two closets upstairs in the additional bedrooms. I might as well take advantage of the space, right? It's not like anybody's going to kick me out."

"You never struck me as someone who would willingly give up your creature comforts, or your walk-in closets."

A shrug and a hint of a smile. "I have two walk-in closets in Logan Creek, but only one in Chicago." The smile spread, mixed with a sigh. "I had to make do."

"Poor you."

"I know, right?" He pointed to the smaller bedroom next to his. "There are a lot of options for this room: an extra bedroom, an office, a den, a TV room." He paused, slipped in another choice. "A nursery."

Vanessa didn't miss the half-second pause or dip in his voice when he mentioned the last possibility. Almost as if he were trying it out to get her reaction, or maybe he'd been gauging his own feelings. A nursery. She pictured pale green walls, white furniture, a crib with a dark-haired baby. She blinked, pushed away visions of a baby with dark hair and dark eyes. Ethan's hair. Ethan's eyes. "Yes," she managed. "So many choices." Were they talking about the room, or were they talking about how they fit into one another's lives?

"Let's head upstairs, so I can show you the other bedrooms. I think you'll like the window seat in the one at the top of the stairs."

Vanessa followed him, grateful for the pause in the conversation. For someone who was known for her insight and deductive reasoning capabilities in the business world, she certainly did not possess this skillset in her personal life, especially where Ethan was concerned. Heavens, she'd given speeches on the subject, received awards and magazine write-ups because of it. Yet, she could not employ any of these qualities to figure out the man behind the mystery. And that was becoming darn frustrating.

"What do you think?" Ethan motioned for her to follow him into the bedroom. "I like the window seat in this one." He moved toward the wooden window seat, glanced out the window. "I always wished I had one when I was a kid. I would have perched right here and waited for the moon and stars to light the sky. And then I would have dragged my pillow and blanket onto the window seat and looked for Orion's Belt, or the Big Dipper, or the North Star." His voice softened. "It would have been magical."

Vanessa studied his profile, wished he'd had the window seat he'd dreamed of so he could spot the constellations. "You're never too old to enjoy the stars." She moved toward the window seat, glanced at the gray sky outside. "It's the perfect view."

"Yes, it is."

The softness in his voice said he was thinking about his childhood dream, but when she turned his gaze was on her. Had she imagined the shift between them or was it real? Could it be that they'd stopped bickering long enough to let down their guard and discover they enjoyed being together? Did he sense it, too? She waited—hoped—he would say something like *Glad you stopped by* or *I like sharing things with you*. Even *Thanks for the cookies*, but his next words said he probably hadn't been thinking about her or them at all.

"You've got to see the bathroom. It's as big as a coat closet, but I'm getting used to it."

"Doubtful."

He laughed, his dark eyes sparkling in a way that made him even more attractive than usual. "True, but I'm working on it. Follow me; it's only three steps down the hall."

The man was not kidding about the three steps or the fact that the bathroom was the size of a coat closet. A very small one.

"There's a basement, too, but nothing exciting other than a washer and dryer, a water heater, and the furnace."

Vanessa homed in on the first part. "A washer and dryer?" She could not resist. "You know what those are?"

A smile spread across his lips. "I do, and I've even been known to use them on occasion, though not often and not well. Come on, I'll show you." She followed him down the stairs to the first level and a door just outside the kitchen. He opened the door, flicked on a light. "Hold onto the railing. The steps are steep."

She grabbed the railing, made her way down the steps. "I'm still searching for the visual of you reading instructions on how to launder a shirt, though I would guess most of your clothing is dry-clean only or hand wash."

He pointed a finger at her. "And what exactly is your point?"

A big sigh and a shake of his head. "Okay, since you know about my handyman abilities, I might as well confess that I actually have someone do my laundry."

"Say it isn't true! Ethan Nance has a laundress?"

He flipped on another light, made his way toward a laundry area equipped with a washer, dryer, and a drying rack. "Laundress is not the term I would use for someone who takes care of the house, makes sure I eat the meals she prepares, and reminds me I'm not the most important person in the world." His voice shifted, filled with tenderness. "Her name's Johanna. No nonsense, German woman. Does not put up with what she calls *foolishness*, especially from me."

"I'd love to meet her. She sounds delightful."

"Yeah, delightful is not exactly the term I'd use to describe Johanna."

But the expression on his face said he didn't mind her spunk. In fact, he liked it. "I'm surprised you're okay with someone keeping you in line." Vanessa ran a hand along the drying rack, wondered what items in Ethan's wardrobe required line drying. "You strike me as the type who doesn't want to hear anything other than your own opinion, and I don't mean that in a bad way because I've heard that about myself as well."

"I do have that tendency, usually because I've dissected the heck out of whatever issue I'm contemplating and I don't trust anyone else to do the same. That's not necessarily a good thing and I'm working on it." His dark gaze settled on her. "Compromise, right?"

"Yes. Compromise." What exactly was he talking about? The space between them heated up, sizzled, and his words suddenly felt *very* personal. Vanessa stepped back, tried to get away from the heat, failed. "So, are you getting any business work done or have you pretty much jumped into full-time remodeling?" What she really wanted to know was if stepping away from the routine of his other life had made him more human and if he'd found a way to balance his business *and* personal life.

"I'm still working and this brain is still synapsing, coming up with ideas and plans. Did you know you can participate in a conference call while you're designing closet shelves and you don't even need to be in a custom-made suit to do it?" He grinned, pointed to the T-shirt and jeans. "You can wear jeans and a T-shirt or a ratty old sweatshirt and forget the hand-stitched shoes. Not necessary. Plus, if you're so inclined, you can toss in a load of laundry—" he pointed to the washer "—or have someone else do it for you. I'm sleeping better than I ever have and spend hours alone in my own form of meditation. I know it sounds crazy, but I'm more relaxed now than I've ever been."

"I get it. How can it be that we can find a way to relax in an unfamiliar environment, doing things that are not in our comfort zone…talking to strangers who feel more like friends? I understand and I've felt that, too. Do you know I've even come up with an idea for a mother-daughter headband project?" She laughed, let the story spill out and the excitement that went with it. "Me, the person who clings to data, has come up with an idea Meredith loves. A *creative* idea, and that is totally unlike me, but it just happened."

He nodded. "I'm not surprised about the creativity part. I spotted it the first time we met." He must have seen her surprise because he added, "You mentioned a few things and I could visualize them. That's creativity."

"I'm not so sure about that..." But there'd been a time when she'd loved to draw and paint and write...before Armand crushed her world.

"Well, *I'm* sure and I want to hear all about your idea." He motioned her toward the steps, followed her up the stairs to the kitchen. "Are you hungry?"

"I could eat." Of course, she was hungry. There'd been a few weeks of queasiness that qualified as her "morning sickness" but that was it. For a person who'd relied on smoothies and yogurt to survive, the idea of eating whole foods was refreshing. Everything she ate or sipped wasn't a shade of green!

"You do eat eggs, right?" When she nodded, he pointed to one of the kitchen chairs and said, "Take a seat and keep me company while I fix you what I bet you'll say is one of the best veggie omelets you've ever eaten."

Vanessa slid into a chair. "Can I slice or dice anything? I'm not much of a cook, but if you provide instructions, I'm happy to help."

He hesitated, then nodded. "You can be in charge of the mushrooms and tomatoes. We'll leave out the onions since they might bother your stomach."

"Thank you." Once again, the man's thoughtfulness surprised and touched her. Ethan removed the mushrooms from the fridge along with a zucchini and a handful of cherry tomatoes. Next came the veggie prep instructions, followed by a conversation on what did and did not constitute cooking ability. Ethan said it involved techniques like sauté, braise, and simmer, while she tried to convince him *ability* was a relative term that could mean heating up or dropping into boiling water.

As they worked on the omelet, a light snow began to fall: pristine, calming, beautiful. Of all the ways Vanessa imagined she might get to know more about the real Ethan Nance, she'd never pictured it would happen in a tiny kitchen with him in a T-shirt and worn-out jeans, dark head bent over an ancient stove as he fixed her a veggie omelet. But it happened and the more they talked, the more they relaxed and Vanessa did what she'd vowed she would never do again: she shared.

Ethan set her plate in front of her, eased into the chair next to hers. "Enjoy."

It had been so long since anyone made a special effort, just for her. "Thank you." Three bites into the omelet, she set down her fork and picked up the slice of wheat toast he'd spread with what he called the most irresistible cherry preserve she'd ever taste. The man had not underestimated the taste. "This is delicious." She munched on the toast, savored the tartness of the cherry preserves. "And the omelet? The mushrooms, zucchini, the tomato...the fluffiness of the egg? It's all perfect. Thank you. It's truly the best omelet I've ever eaten." *Because you made it*, she almost added. *Because you showed me you cared and no one's done that in a long time*. She couldn't tell him that because it might be just a bit too much truth right now, so she added, "You'd better be careful because if you show this side of yourself, every woman will be after you." Her stomach flip-flopped the second she spoke the words. She did not want to think about all of the women who already found him attractive, or the ones who would now add him to their list.

"I'm very selective about who I share my culinary talents with... In fact, I've never cooked for any woman before."

"Never? Oh, then why...?"

His gaze burned into her, his voice rough when he spoke. "Guess I never wanted to before."

## 17

I t had been years since a woman captivated Ethan's interest, but Vanessa had done it without even trying. In fact, she'd tried to dismiss his relevance in regard to their baby, and in regard to *her*. Good luck with that.

Ethan wasn't deserting his child and if Vanessa stayed in Reunion Gap, then he would, too. If she moved to Nebraska, he'd find a place there. The point was, she was not getting rid of him. He might not have ever pictured himself as a father, but now that he was going to be one, he would be a good one—*a present one*—not the kind who disappeared or no-showed, like his own father.

But it wasn't just about the baby and Ethan couldn't ignore or deny that truth any longer. It was also about Vanessa. The woman confused and unsettled him as much as she mesmerized and intrigued him. She was no doubt the greatest challenge he'd ever faced and the most impossible to understand, but the last few hours with her had felt good, right, normal—and he wanted a chance for more.

He supposed washing and drying dishes together could be classified as a "normal" event. Ethan wouldn't know since he'd never engaged in that sort of task before with a female companion. No, he'd been careful to keep "companions" away from his personal space, but Vanessa was different. *She* mattered. He set a plate in the drying rack, glanced at her. "You really don't have to dry these dishes. We could let them air-dry."

She shrugged, picked up the plate, began drying it. "I know, but I want to..."

"So, confession. I know how to wash dishes. I'm very familiar with the vacuum cleaner, though I haven't used one in years. And I used to change the oil in my car but it's been a while."

That made her smile. "I'm pretty sure the cars you drive these days require a bit of special handling."

Obviously, she'd heard about the Ferrari and she'd seen the Mercedes the other day.

He tossed her a smile, followed it with a laugh. "True."

"I thought so." She raised a brow. "A Ferrari *and* a Mercedes?"

"Yes, well... You know, there's a reason for this overblown ego and arrogance. I'd like to blame it on my mother, but I definitely had a hand in it."

Humor spilled through her next words. "You don't say?"

The lightheartedness in her tone made him want to tell her more. When had he *ever* wanted to do that? Right. Never. Until now. "My mother taught me the art of thinking I was the only person in the world who mattered and I deserved the best, even if we couldn't afford it. Even if I really didn't deserve it. My father wasn't in the picture. He took off before I ever got to know him, and my mother spent years trying to make up for it: spending money, filling my head with *You're so wonderful*, making me believe I could have anything I wanted just because I existed." He rinsed another dish, handed it to her. "What kid wouldn't pick the autographed football over the store one? And the fancy tennis shoes. I mean, when everything is up for grabs and you're told to just pick the one you like best? But then one day I opened my eyes and found a collection notice. That torpedoed the reality: we couldn't afford our lifestyle and I had to fix that."

"Oh, Ethan...I'm so sorry."

A shrug, and an almost laugh. "Hey, maybe that turned me into the control freak I am today. If I hadn't lived through that I'd probably be doing something like teaching English or building houses. Instead, I figure out ways to help people make their businesses profitable and attractive to a customer or an investor. It's all about strategy and not just numbers or spread-sheets but analyzing, anticipating, and implementing. I can see it all like a chess match as I calculate my opponent's next five moves. I'm usually right because I study the board, consider every possibility." He glanced at her, held her gaze. "But I never saw you coming." Vanessa opened her mouth to speak but he stopped her. "The damn problem is, I still haven't figured out what to do about it."

"I see." She looked away, clamped her mouth shut and began drying a fork.

What had she expected him to say? *I never saw you coming but I'm glad you did. I never pictured a baby in my life but I'm glad there is one and I'm glad you're the mother. I want you to be the mother of my child and I want so much more?* How could he say any of those things when he didn't know what he thought because his brain was one big jumble? If he listened to emotion, he'd pull her in his arms right now and kiss her, vow to give them a chance. But he hadn't let emotion rule his decisions in a very long time, not since he lost Darcy.

"I think maybe I should go." She folded the dishtowel, set it on the drainboard. "Thank you for a very enjoyable day." The smile did not look genuine. "And for the omelet."

"Wait." He reached out, placed a hand on her forearm. "You

know, I'm great at developing and fostering business relationships. I can even show others how to do it and *why* it makes
perfect sense. But a personal relationship? One-on-one? Well,
I'm a massive fail in that area, except for Daniel and he doesn't
count because he's my best friend."

Those hazel eyes narrowed on him. "Why are you telling me
this?"

Why *was* he telling her truths he'd never shared with anyone
else? "Because opening up and spitting out emotion isn't in my
DNA but I did it today and I can't even say why."

"Because you wanted to...? Because you knew I wouldn't
judge? Maybe because you felt safe with me?"

The shimmer in her eyes said she wanted to believe all of
those possibilities and she wanted him to admit to them. But he
couldn't because that would make him much too vulnerable, so
he offered another choice. "Or maybe because I wanted you to
understand why I'm not the guy who believes in ever-after."

A nod, a tight "I see. Well, no worries from me. It's not like
we're interested in a relationship other than as parents. I mean,
what would that even look like? We're both afraid to trust, not
interested in sharing, and we are never going to—"

Ethan pulled her to him, blocked the rest of her words with a
kiss filled with passion, desperation, and longing...so damn much
longing. He'd dreamed of touching her again, kissing her,
stroking her soft flesh. Her whimpers of pleasure filled him,
made him want to taste every inch of her body, sink himself
inside... *Damn!* He broke the kiss, stepped back, swallowed.
"I'm sorry. I shouldn't have done that."

She stared at him, lips glistening from their kiss, eyes
narrowed on him as if she wanted to burrow into his brain and
find answers to questions he didn't understand. "If you didn't
want me here, why did you invite me to stay? And if you don't
share, why did you tell me about your mother and your difficult

upbringing?" She fisted her hands on her hips, glared. "Why didn't you keep it all buried beneath that cool exterior that says, 'I don't want anybody and I don't need anybody?'" The tiny nostrils flared, the lips pinched. "Or is that a convenient line you keep in your pickup arsenal?"

He scowled, dragged a hand through his hair. Now she was being ridiculous. "I've never used a pickup line and if I did, trust me, it would not be that one."

"I hope not because it's pathetic." She strode past him, grabbed her handbag and was two steps from the living room when he spoke.

"Pathetic but true."

Vanessa swung around, stared. "What did you say?"

Ethan let out a deep sigh, almost wished he'd kept his mouth shut. Could nothing be easy or familiar with this woman? Did every single thing have to be buried in arguments and complications? An hour ago, they'd been laughing and discussing the definition of cooking skills, and then he'd opened his big mouth and the dynamics had shifted, turned to stone and landed on his chest. Why couldn't she—

"Forget it. I'm leaving."

And then she was in the living room, shrugging into her coat.

"Vanessa." Ethan moved toward her, tried to find the words to express the jumble going on in his head and damn it, his heart. "I like you and I don't want to hurt you."

"Then don't," she said, her voice soft, eyes bright.

It wasn't that simple; couldn't she see that? "But I don't know if I can give you what you deserve." *Love, happiness, a life filled with joy.*

"Because you can't or because you won't? That's what you should be thinking about. Aren't you the chess player who can see five moves ahead? Well, consider the value behind those moves." She tightened the belt on her coat, offered a tight smile.

"Do you want to win the game and destroy every chance for happiness with it because you were afraid to take the risk?"

Ethan blinked. Had she really just labeled him *afraid*? His jaw twitched, twitched again. "I've never met anyone like you and that's created a huge problem for me."

"I'll bet it has." The lips he'd kissed minutes ago turned into a cold smile. "Why don't you re-think those chess moves you plan to make, see if they're worth it?" The smile spread, turned colder. "When you've figured it out, give me a call. Until then, leave me alone."

## 18

Snow had a way of revitalizing a person, jolting him awake from his day-to-day routines and thought processes. And walking in the stuff? That was better than a triple espresso and pure magic to the senses. After yesterday's commentary from Vanessa about re-thinking his chess moves or leaving her alone, he'd been agitated, grouchy, definitely ticked. He'd tried to be honest and what did that honesty get him?

A lecture on what not to do and what not to think. And she had the gall to say he was afraid? *Afraid of what, exactly?* Should he *want* to give someone the power to control his moods, his choices, his happiness? Why would he choose to be in a constant state of upheaval and uncertainty because he couldn't protect the other person or protect himself from losing them? No, *just no.*

He would not apologize for refusing to bungee jump into a relationship with a questionable harness. In his experience, it was better to observe from the sidelines and run the actuarial tables on success versus failure. That made sense to him. That was the safer bet and a way to hedge destruction and grief.

What was so wrong with that? Yes, a person might be a spectator and the sidelines weren't the same as participating, but at least there wouldn't be broken bones—definitely not broken hearts.

Apparently, Vanessa didn't see it that way, though she hadn't come straight out and said she wanted a relationship with him. No, she'd danced around the subject, coming in sideways with comments about *chess moves* and *winning the game* and *losing everything*. Sure, he got it. Commit to something other than a spreadsheet and a business plan or don't touch her. Fine. Why had he gone and kissed her anyway? That was foolish and just because they'd had a great day talking and—*gag*—sharing did not mean that was his new persona. Absolutely not. Who could say why he'd opened his mouth and spat out the tale of his pathetic backstory or the mother who thought he was her little king?

Ethan trudged through the snow toward downtown, his aggravation escalating with each step. Why the hell *had* he kissed her? He knew better. Never kiss a woman you can't walk away from... Daniel would call him crazy for that thought, but that's because he was so deep in love with his wife, he probably didn't remember back when he'd felt the same way. The kiss had just happened and again, that was a problem. The same problem that had landed them in bed and ended with Vanessa pregnant.

So, what was *the problem*? Ethan considered all of the possibilities, and a few he hadn't entertained before.

*She was unique.*

*She was the most beautiful woman he'd ever met.*

*She possessed an IQ that mirrored his.*

*She wore a perfume with a pheromone that proved irresistible.*

*She was a challenge.*

*She was a miracle sent to rescue him.*

*She was not impressed with his style, intelligence, or wit.*

*She was as untrusting as he was.*
*She wanted him.*
*She didn't want him.*
*She was a mystery.*

He played around with a few scenarios, dismissed most of them, and vowed to push her out of his mind for the next hour or two as he strolled through town, visited the Cherry Top Diner for a bowl of chili and a hunk of sourdough bread, and then headed to Oliver Donovan's record shop. The man was old school, classic rock 'n' roll and Ethan wanted a chance to peruse the vinyls on his shelves. When he entered the shop, the bell above the door tinkled his presence, but it was the French bulldog charging at him that brought Oliver Donovan from the back room.

"Maybelline! Leave it." The dog screeched to a stop, sat and began wagging her tail. "Good girl. Good girl." The man he'd heard had once played keyboard in a band and toured the country approached him, offered a smile. "Ethan, nice to see you." He glanced past him at the falling snow outside. "If this keeps up, we'll see six inches or more by morning."

Ethan kept his gaze on Oliver's dog who eyed him as though trying to decide if she should obey her master or go with her instincts and lunge. The whimper said he might be safe for now. "Snow doesn't seem to keep people down around here. They just shovel it or plow it out of the way and go about their business."

The nod made the man's ponytail bounce back and forth. "The residents of Reunion Gap are a resilient bunch. Not much keeps us down, especially with Christmas just around the corner." He let out a sigh, rubbed his stubbled jaw. "It can get hectic, but this place is really special around the holidays." He paused, homed in on Ethan with the same intentness as his dog. "Will you be here for Christmas?"

What to say to that one? "That's the plan." But what he

didn't share was that Christmas hadn't meant anything to him in a long time and he'd always spent it working. That was his comfort zone: just his thoughts, his spreadsheets, and his computer. He'd tried the "getting away" version of avoiding Christmas, which included jetting to a luxury resort with or without a companion. The solo trip proved more relaxing than the plus-one: no pouty expressions when he wasn't in the mood for a fancy dinner or excursion, no endless chatter, no constant attempts to get his attention or try to keep it when they did get it. No expectations. If he went solo, he could read, enjoy a quiet meal and a fine scotch, get a hot stone massage...read more...work on next year's business plan. It always came back to work, and the absolute knowing he would not put himself at risk to lose anything again—especially his heart and there was great—

"Did you know your girlfriend likes dogs?"

"What?" Ethan stepped away from the French bulldog, brushed his slacks. "She's not my girlfriend."

The man who definitely saw too much raised a brow, the expression on his tanned face curious. "Okay then... Baby mama? Partner? Associate?"

"How about just Vanessa?"

"Vanessa," Oliver Donovan repeated. "Beautiful name for a beautiful woman."

"Right." No use denying the obvious. A person only had to take a two-second look to notice, and once she began to speak, they'd see that she was—

"...intelligent, witty, engaging," Oliver continued, rubbing his unshaven jaw. "But she's got a protective shell thicker than a stone crab. Hmm." More jaw rubbing, a quiet "Why do you suppose that is?"

Ethan had been wondering about that himself, but Mr. I-can-solve-anything hadn't been able to collect enough data to formulate a plausible reason. A shrug, followed by "No idea, other than she doesn't want to get hurt or she's been hurt and not going to get hurt again."

The older man narrowed his blue gaze on Ethan. "Sounds about right." And then he offered a bit of seemingly unrelated information. "You know she's a fan of Neil Diamond and vinyl."

No, of course he hadn't known she liked that particular singer *or* vinyl, but if he thought about it, well, it made sense. The glimpses of the woman revealed through these references made sense. "Precision is important to her, and I've read that vinyl still provides the most authentic sound. As for Neil Diamond, I could see where the man's lyrics might resonate with her."

"You mean lyrics that struggle for answers and ask the hard questions?" Oliver motioned him toward the counter and the old-school memorabilia crowding it. "Yeah, I could see where she might be attuned to some hard life lessons and getting through the rough times."

Ethan picked up a comic book, studied it. "She's been spending time here and I'm curious about that." His gaze shifted to Oliver, tried to read his expression. Why was Vanessa hanging around with this guy? The man might look like a worn-out rock-'n'-roller with his ponytail, faded jeans, graphic T-shirt, and earring, and that might well be one's initial assumption. Unless a person were to look beyond the obvious for the truth, which beat like a drum riff—if one were half listening. The man possessed a keen intelligence, extreme patience, and the ability to assess a situation *and* a solution, and if a person were paying attention, he'd notice that Oliver Donovan was a listener who didn't judge, advise, *or* lecture.

And maybe that's why Vanessa visited this place—it provided clarity during a confusing time. Hmm. Maybe Ethan could use a bit of clarity, too, and it would appear this man could be just the person to deliver it.

"So, you want to know why she comes here and you don't want to ask her, does that sound about right?" When Ethan nodded, Oliver pinned him with that blue gaze that would make a less confident man look away. "I'm not a preacher, a psychologist, or an adviser, but I know how to listen. It wasn't always that way, but I've finally figured out one or two things. If you listen, people talk. That's how it is with me and Vanessa. She drops in, I fix her a smoothie and offer whatever sweet I've baked." He paused, worked up a slow smile. "She's partial to my double fudge brownies, but she likes the chocolate macadamia-nut cookies, too." More smiling, coupled with a laugh. "One day she ate three brownies."

"Three brownies? You did say double fudge, correct? Real brownies, real sugar?"

A raised brow, a chuckle. "Is there any other kind?"

"Interesting." And confusing. She'd nibbled one of the dark chocolate cookies yesterday, barely finished it. If she loved her sugar fixes, why not admit it? Why couldn't she just be herself around him...whoever that was?

"Ethan?"

"Huh?"

Oliver pointed to the comic book in his hand. "How about you go easy on that book? Customers won't go for one that's torn and tattered."

"Sure. Sorry." Ethan tried to smooth out the semi-wrinkled comic book, eased it back into the display section.

"So, about Vanessa. A person can say a lot without ever speaking, or when they do say something, it's often the spaces between the words that can tell you everything. That's how it is with Vanessa. Ever notice that?"

"Of course, I've noticed." But it was difficult to look for the spaces between the words when there weren't any words...or there weren't enough of them to recognize a pattern. "I'm just trying to understand what's going on here. Can you fill me in?"

"Here, as in what's going on in my record shop?" His blue eyes narrowed. "Or here, as in what's going on between you and Vanessa?"

# 19

It had been nine days since "the kiss." Desire, need, passion...it was all tied into those few seconds when reality meshed with possibility and he'd forgotten why he could never open up to a woman again. Then it was over, leaving him stunned and unable to decipher not only what had happened—but why. That's when he'd blown up the possibility of "real" with comments about his inability to commit to a "relationship." Stupid. Idiotic. But he'd spoken the words and expected her to accept or at least understand them. But what had she done? Vanessa had turned iceberg cold *and* she'd accused him of being afraid of a relationship. Afraid! Damn but he detested that word.

Since their "falling out," the effort to deny he cared about her had grown exhausting, stolen his ability to formulate a thought that did not begin and end with Vanessa. Oliver Donovan had given him a lot to think about the afternoon Ethan wandered into his store, tossing out questions in a casual, nonjudgmental way.

*Are you interested in a relationship with Vanessa?*

*A real one, not a "for now" or "as long as it feels right"?*

*Can you commit?*

*Do you want to make this work?*

*What about trust? Can you share the less-than flattering parts of yourself?*

*Could you love her?*

And then the big one, *Do you love her?*

The questions spun through his head for days, swirling so fast they landed him with more than one headache. Unfortunately, the answers weren't as easy to detect, especially when Ethan did not want to admit the huge stumbling block to clarity. He *was* afraid! That was not a welcome or comfortable acknowledgment and it took a solid forty-eight hours to accept, but the truth was the truth and it was time to tell her.

Vanessa Rodelle had taken residence in his brain, his psyche, his blasted soul. The woman could burn him with a look, and when she coupled that with a few well-placed lines, she knew exactly how to confuse and frustrate him. Nobody had ever been able to do that with such accuracy and consistency, but she sure did. He didn't like it, and yet there didn't seem to be a damn thing he could do about it. And he'd tried. Oh yes, he'd employed all sorts of tactics that ranged from attempting to convince himself he was only interested in her as the mother of his child, labeling her as a challenge to be overcome or a puzzle to be solved, even classifying her as a temporary "imbalance" to his organized life. And the classic fail that he employed after "the kiss" when he told her he wasn't capable of *ever* committing to a woman.

After several nights of careful dissection, he recognized that comment as straight-up fear. He needed to tell her and that's what landed him outside of her room at the Peace & Harmony Inn. Uncertain, anxious. Hopeful. None of those words belonged in his vocabulary, yet here they were, pulsing through him like a heartbeat.

Did she feel the same way? Would she want to give them—

"What are you doing here? Please leave."

Vanessa stood on the other side of the door: unsmiling, tense, more beautiful than the last time he saw her. Her eyes were bright, glistening. Were those tears? If so, why? He should be able to assess and categorize, but he couldn't. The woman had confused him since the first time they met...long before that. Maybe since their first conversation, and he was done pretending he didn't want her for way more than the mother of his child. This wasn't about a challenge or a puzzle or anything other than Vanessa. It was about *them* and what they could be together. "You want me to leave?" *Say it. Say the words.*

She licked her lips, held his gaze. "I think you should leave," she repeated.

Answering without answering. Ethan did recognize that response as one stuffed with fear. He pushed past his own uncertainty *and* fear, offered up the truth. "I *should* leave, no doubt about it. I've been a jerk, a fool, and an idiot." He dragged a hand through his hair, desperate to get her to listen. "You called me afraid and you were right. I *was* afraid to open up to you, to admit there was something special between us—" he held her gaze, willed her to understand "—to admit I wanted more." A sigh, a clearing of his throat. "Doing that would make me too vulnerable, too exposed, much too dependent on you. It would force me to trust you in ways I haven't had to do in a very long time...if ever."

A tear slipped onto her left cheek, trailed to her neck. Were those happy tears? Sad tears? Or sorry-you're-too-late tears? Ethan waited for her to say something, *anything*, but she remained silent, those hazel eyes threatening more tears. He could not give up yet, not until she told him with actual words that he was too late. Even then, he might not stop trying to convince her to give him a chance to prove how right they could be.

"I want to be with you, Vanessa, and not just because of the baby." He tried for a smile, but it fell flat. "I haven't thought about the baby since you opened the door." His gaze slid to her stomach, inched back to her face. "That doesn't mean I don't care about this baby because I do—very much. What it means is that I also care about the baby's mother."

She shook her head, stepped back as if to get away from his words. "How do I know these aren't just 'for now' words? I've never met anyone who could speak with such eloquence or conviction as you. You're a master at it, placing just the right tone and inflection depending on what narrative you're pushing."

How could he make her believe he meant what he said? Yes, he possessed the talent of persuasion and yes, he'd used it many times to gain a particular outcome. This was different; this was *real*. "Vanessa, I'm telling you the truth. I want to be with you and I'll do whatever I need to...including the whole sharing business."

"Sharing business?" Those hazel eyes sliced him. "Okay, so you're willing to share and you might even believe you *want* to be with me. You might even use words like *commitment* and *relationship*, but what about next week or ten weeks from now? Will you still feel that way?" Her expression turned fierce. "You confuse me, Ethan, and I can't have people or situations I can't depend on in my life."

"You can depend on me," he blurted out, desperate to get her to give him a chance. "Let me show you." And then because he had no idea what else to say, he ended with "Please?" She stared at him, eyes wide and filled with tears, jaw clenched. Maybe she needed time, or maybe she really *didn't* want a chance at a life with him. If the first were the case, he'd give her as much time as she needed. However, if it were the latter, then she was going to say the words. "Tell me you don't want me in your life as anything other than the baby's father. Say the words, Vanessa. I need to hear them."

He cleared his throat, forced out more truths before she shut him down. "If you do want me in your life, no doubt it's going to get messy at times. But the first time I spotted you across the room, it got messy because you were like no one I'd ever met." Opening his heart was terrifying but even a nonbeliever like him could acknowledge the potential rewards. "So, tell me what you want."

Now it was up to her. This was the part about trusting someone he didn't like. Ethan wanted to control his own journey, but sometimes that wasn't possible, not if you wanted a *relationship*, which apparently his addled brain and heart did. Five seconds passed, then eight, twelve as he waited for her answer.

Vanessa opened her mouth, closed it. Stared. Said nothing, which told him everything. He'd muddled the opportunity when she'd offered it and now it was too late. She'd decided he wasn't worth the risk. Okay, got it. No words necessary, not with the frozen expression plastering her face and the eyes that couldn't make their way past his chin. Fine. He understood. Ethan had gambled on an unknown, something he *never* did, and lost. "Okay then. I'll see you at the next doctor visit." A nod and one more glance at the woman who'd burrowed into his brain *and* his heart. "Take care." And then he turned and headed toward the stairway, desperate to get outside, suck in air that was not saturated with her hyacinth-lavender scent.

"Stay."

Ethan stopped, turned to face her. "What did you say?"

She moved toward him, repeated in a voice so soft he could barely hear, "Stay."

Stay. *Stay.* He closed the distance between them, consumed with that one word that meant everything. She wanted to be with him, *wanted him*! Ethan framed her face with his hands, leaned in and placed a gentle kiss on her mouth: hopeful, reverent, honest. Tonight was a new beginning for them, one marked with discoveries, sharing, real joy. "Vanessa," he murmured against her lips.

Her hands wound around his neck, pulled him closer. And then she whispered the words he'd dreamed of hearing since the first time they made love. "Take me to bed."

AFTER THAT NIGHT WITH ETHAN, life changed in a way Vanessa had never believed possible. The world opened up, grew brighter, filled with laughter, hope, possibility—with Ethan and their child. But it wasn't the fact that they were having a baby together that marked the change. No, it was the sharing and conversations in and out of bed.

When he spoke, he didn't seem to feel the need to always be on point, perfect, precise. He used words that didn't imply all-knowing, and there'd been a few times when he'd even expressed uncertainty. For a man like Ethan, that was a huge admission. It made Vanessa feel close to him as though he trusted her and was learning to be comfortable showing his true self, the one behind the designer suits, the spreadsheets, the fancy cars. They took long walks, strategized over ways Langston Turnings and Passion Plan to Success could work together on various programs. They even began cooking together. Who would have ever thought Vanessa would *want* to spend time in the kitchen? Ethan had a knack for it though one would never guess from his business presence. The man not only knew the difference between braised and sautéed but how to create it. Last night, he fixed the most perfect chicken dish, fed it to her as she sat on his lap.

Goodness, she would have bet her entire portfolio no man would *ever* feed her from his fork while she sat on his lap and that man would certainly *not* be Ethan Nance. Surprises weren't always bad ones and she was learning that step by step. And the physical attraction? Oh, that was breathtaking and *breath stealing*. Ethan knew how to please a woman, how to make her feel as though she were all that mattered...as though she were his world. Who wouldn't want *that*? But the talking that came afterward moved her as much as his lovemaking. She knew that kind of sharing was as new and rare to him as it was to her, and that said *special*.

Vanessa had never believed she'd meet a man she could trust again, one she'd want to share her life with, but she'd never met anyone like Ethan. Soon she would tell him about her past, the family she'd been born into, the estranged relationship with them and the reason behind it. Yes, if they were going to have a future together—and it certainly looked as if they would—she had to be honest about everything, including the parts she'd wanted to bury. It was important to show him all of her, including the messed-up parts. In time, he'd do the same.

Meredith gushed all over Vanessa every time they were together. *I'll bet he's going to ask you to marry him soon. What kind of wedding would you like? Small? Huge? Destination?* Talk of weddings and marriage made Vanessa queasy. She and Ethan were still getting to know one another, beginning to trust one another, and it was much too soon to think about marriage. The first time she'd said "I do," those vows had been tied to treachery and betrayal.

Could she risk that again? Would Ethan even *want* to venture into marriage?

That was a lifetime commitment—or should be—and it should not be rushed. For now, it was enough to concentrate on being together and learning about one another and the baby. The mistakes and regrets of the past could wait a while longer. But a few days later, the opportunity presented itself for Vanessa to share the sad story of her disastrous first marriage and she couldn't avoid it. Rather, she didn't *want* to avoid it because she'd come to trust Ethan more than she'd ever trusted any other man—including Armand, her ex-husband. She and Ethan were sharing a shrimp and risotto meal he'd prepared along with salads and sparkling water. Ethan didn't seem at all bothered that he'd given up alcohol, which included his favorite scotch, for the remainder of the pregnancy. *It seems fair. You've given it up, so can I. It's the least I can do.* Who would have thought such kindness and concern existed beneath that cool exterior? And who would have thought she'd be drawn to—

"There's been a lot of chatter around town regarding an unlikely couple."

"Oh? Is it about Oliver and Jennifer?" She hoped the two were finally making it official, telling the world and each other they wanted to spend the rest of their lives together.

Ethan shook his head. "Nope, this is about Carter, the one who favors twenty-somethings and got one pregnant a while back. I heard he had a baby, can't remember the sex of the child, but word has it the woman's pressuring for a ring. He's stalling but sounds like he won't be able to stall much longer."

The tone in his voice made her wonder if there was a question buried in his words. "She wants a ring because he's the father of her child?" Did he think she wanted one, too—because she was having his baby? Vanessa toyed with her fork, waited for his answer.

A sigh, a shift in his chair. "My guess is she's been after him long before there was a baby. Word has it he's been playing house with other women for years." Another sigh. "And he finally got caught. Still, it's a big commitment, one that can turn upside down fast if the guy doesn't go in with his eyes wide open."

"Meaning, he needs to understand the not-so-exciting part of being with someone every day?"

His gaze narrowed the tiniest bit. "Right."

Did he think she'd pressure him? No, he wouldn't think that. But just in case, she offered her thoughts. "People jump into marriage for all the wrong reasons, looking for happiness, trying to find what's missing in their life, a surprise pregnancy, a way out of a life they don't like." Visions of the arguments with her parents blew through her brain, settled in her soul. "It never works; there's always some sort of collateral damage."

"Collateral damage?"

"Of course. A couple gets married for the wrong reason or even for the right reason and if they're not 100 percent in, it ends in disaster. If children are involved, watch the tug-of-war fireworks. No children doesn't mean no problems. What do you do with the friends? Who gets them? And what about the parents who might or might not have condoned the marriage? If the couple splits, does the bride admit to her parents that they were right all along?" Her voice grew louder, bordered on frantic. "That she should have listened to them, should not have jumped into a situation with a man she only *thought* she knew?" She'd buried her feelings for so long, they poured out before she could yank them back.

"Vanessa? Are you okay?"

A tear slid down her cheek, escaped to her chin. She sniffed, continued, "Does she bury her pride and the dreams she once had and follow their rules for the rest of her life? When she learns he's only married her for money and the prestige that comes along with it, what should she do? How can she move past that to a belief that men *do* exist who aren't interested in the family name or the money and power that go with it? How can she ever believe they might actually be interested in *her*?" Her voice cracked, split open with pain. "She can't accept it. All of the failings and the way he's used her and the money he's taken. The betrayal. The humiliation. The pain. It's all too much." She swiped at another tear. "So, she does the only thing she knows how to do. She builds a wall so no one can hurt her again and she *pretends*. Yes, she pretends she doesn't care, doesn't want a chance at happiness or a life full of joy because she now believes it doesn't exist. Not for her."

"Vanessa?"

She blinked through her tears, cleared her throat. "Yes?"

"Tell me what that jerk did to you. I want to know everything."

## 20

W hen Vanessa shared her past with Ethan, she didn't miss the hard set of his jaw or the way his gaze narrowed as though he might punch the man if he were in the room. And she definitely didn't mistake his eerie stillness. He asked questions about her family: who they were, what they meant to her, the relationship they once had. And he asked about her ex-husband. Last name along with the timeframe when he inserted himself into her life. *How did he approach you? Did you know his friends? Where did he live? Did he pay with cash or credit cards? Do you remember any of the places you went? What city? What line of work did he claim to have? Do you have any idea where he is now?* And then, the question she'd often wondered herself, *What's the likelihood he's still preying on the naïve and unsuspecting?*

She had no idea where he was or what he was doing. Once the divorce became final and her parents had paid off his debts and given him an outrageous sum of money, he disappeared. However, his parting included a smile she now recognized as devious and arrogant and the words, *It was nothing personal, Vanessa. I hope you understand. I do care about you. This is just business. I would have remained married to you if your parents hadn't stepped in and shut things down.* Another smile, this one more sickening than the last. *We were good together. You know that. If you ever want to have fun, I'll be around.*

How could she have lived with this secret for so long, never telling a soul aside from her estranged parents what she'd done, the mistakes and bad choices she'd made? She'd been manipulated and betrayed, but not without her permission. Once she told Ethan, she felt free and wanted to share her story with Meredith, who'd known her own grief, misfortune, and betrayal. For a little while, they'd all believed Daniel Reese was yet another heartbreak and betrayal for Meredith, but he'd surprised them all when he revealed his true identity and love for Meredith in a gallery showing. *That* was true love. *That* was honesty and devotion, and while somewhat misguided and messed up in the beginning, it had found its way to the truth and ever after. The day Daniel proclaimed his love for Meredith in front of cameras and microphones, Vanessa began to wonder if true love did still exist.

And now Ethan was in her life and she asked herself that same question as she lay beside him each night, woke next to him each morning: did true love still exist? And then her heart would whisper the only question she really wanted to know: *Could it exist with Ethan?* He was a complicated man, but he'd opened up with her in ways she doubted he'd ever done with anyone before...maybe not even with his best friend, Daniel. Certainly not with a woman. The more they were together, the more sides of him she saw and that only made him more desirable. It might take a lifetime to piece together the extraordinarily complex persona of Ethan Nance and maybe she *wanted* that lifetime—with him. They hadn't talked about a long-term relationship, but what did that really mean other than spending time together, enjoying one another's company—the physical and non-physical aspects—both of which she enjoyed far more than she wanted to admit.

There were no labels or discussions about their future or what it might look like aside from the co-parent aspects. But what about a future with Ethan? Could he ever commit to an all-in relationship with her? Her heart beat faster when she thought of the possibility and only a fool would continue to pretend the answer didn't matter.

And Vanessa had never been a fool. She cared about Ethan Nance, probably too much, and that made her vulnerable. But if he cared about her, too, then wasn't that where joy and ever-after stepped in?

THE PHONE CALL that changed Vanessa's life came late one afternoon as she moved paint swatches around on the kitchen table, matching shades of green, blue, and pink. Who would have thought selecting an accent color for a baby's room would prove so challenging? Ethan favored teal but thought the lime green would also be a good choice. *But only if it's a boy*, he'd said in a gentle voice, placing his hand on her belly. *A girl needs pink, at least some version of it.*

Yes, a girl did need pink. She eased five swatches of "pink" next to the ivory swatch. Perfect peony, palest rose, pure pink, soft blush, pink carnation. There were so many choices when the main color was ivory and maybe she would take Meredith's advice and pick up small jars of paint and brush them on the wall next to each other. Actually, Ethan would be the one doing the painting since he didn't want her near the stuff.

It would be so much easier if they knew the sex of the baby *before* the delivery, but they'd decided to wait. Not that either *wanted* to wait. Oh no, they certainly didn't. Why would individuals obsessed with planning and organization opt *not* to know? The answer was pretty simple once you considered the entire scope of the situation. They had a unique opportunity to present each other with a gift—*the gift of anticipation.* There was nothing quite like wondering, hoping, dreaming...

*Anticipating.*

Of course, Ethan vowed once the baby was born, he'd have the room painted and complete before they were discharged from the hospital. Vanessa didn't challenge that comment, but merely smiled and nodded. Either Ethan had no idea how exhausted *he* might be after the delivery or he planned to hire a painter. Hmm. She'd have to pose that question to him tonight over dinner. But the phone call that came as she contemplated color swatches and tonight's dinner changed everything. It stole her appetite, her peace of mind, injected shreds of anxiety and apprehension that would not be appeased until she met the caller on the other end of the line.

"Hello. Is this Vanessa?"

"Yes." Vanessa didn't recognize the woman's voice but she did detect the class and culture in it.

"My name is Rebecca Nance. I'm Ethan's mother."

"Oh. Mrs. Nance. Hello." Why was the woman calling her when Ethan had made no mention of telling his mother about them *or* the baby?

"Rebecca, dear. It's much less formal, more intimate. And after all, we are going to be family, aren't we?"

"I..." Did she know about the baby?

A small laugh, a clearing of her throat and a thrum of excitement flitted through the line. "My son doesn't know I'm calling, so please don't tell him. Not until you and I meet."

"Are you coming to Reunion Gap?" Did she plan to surprise Ethan? Something told Vanessa it would not be a welcome surprise and keeping this phone call from him would be worse.

"No, not yet, though I had hoped you would travel to his hometown so we could meet and have a very important conversation… One that should be held here." There was the slightest hesitation followed by "You see, my son is my life and I would do anything for him. I don't want to see him hurt again. Gracious, I don't think he could stand it."

*Again?* What did that mean? "I don't understand."

"No, of course you don't. That's why I'd like you to visit so I can tell you everything about my son, even the parts he undoubtedly left out."

"Mrs. Nance—Rebecca—I don't think Ethan would want me to keep this from him. Why is it so important to do that?"

"I'm not asking you to keep it from him forever…just until after we meet." The tiniest sigh filled with what sounded like hope. "After that, I do so hope we'll spend time together. And when the baby comes… How wonderful will that be? I have so longed to be a grandmother."

Vanessa clutched the phone, tried to understand what was happening. "Did Ethan tell you about the baby?"

"No, he did not." A laugh, a long breath of air. "My son doesn't tell me much of anything about his private life other than to insist he's happy, doing what he wants to do, living the life intended for him." Pause followed by a soft "But a mother always knows her children. I hear the sadness and the longing in his voice when he speaks, but not this last time. It was different; I heard notes of what I can only describe as real joy. When I found out about you and the baby, then it all made sense." Pleasure seeped through the line, landed in Vanessa's lap. "Ethan wants you and the baby…*he wants a family*. How wonderful is that?"

Vanessa sipped air, tried to remain calm as she attempted to figure out who had delivered information to Ethan's mother. "If Ethan didn't tell you about me and the baby, then who did?"

Who else even knew his mother? Daniel? He wouldn't do it, and Meredith had learned her lesson about nosing around where it wasn't her business. Hadn't she?

"I'm sorry but I gave my word that I wouldn't divulge that information, not until you visited. Please, don't worry. This person assured me this was done as a service to you and my son."

*Who could it be?* "Can you at least tell me if it was one of Ethan's friends?" Though once Vanessa spoke, she realized the only friend she'd ever heard Ethan mention was Daniel.

"Forgive me, I can't divulge that information until we meet. Please come as soon as possible so you can understand the parts of my son's life he's left out. They're painful and for years he's tried to ignore them and pretend they don't matter, but they do. If you're going to have a life with him, which I hope you will, then you need to know the whole Ethan Nance—not just the one he shows you."

"I can be there tomorrow."

"Wonderful. I'll send directions."

When the phone call ended, Vanessa ran to the bathroom and threw up the egg salad on rye she'd eaten for lunch. The very last thing she wanted to do was keep secrets from Ethan, but apparently, his mother wasn't going to share this "essential information" about her son unless Vanessa remained quiet. Once she visited Rebecca Nance, then she would tell Ethan everything.

If hearing about the sad parts of his life, along with the painful ones, helped their relationship, then she'd do it—for Ethan and for what they could be together. Did she want to do it? No, absolutely not, but as she was learning, relationships often required a person to do things they didn't want to do. When Ethan arrived home late that afternoon, he must have noticed something wasn't right.

"Are you not feeling well?" He touched her forehead, frowned. "What's wrong?"

There was such concern on his face that she almost told him and later she would wish she had, but she held back, blamed the egg salad on rye that didn't sit well in her stomach. What she neglected to add was the reason. Ethan fixed her dry toast, sat with her, rubbed her back and shoulders, murmured *Everything will be better in the morning. You'll see.*

## 21

Ethan's hometown was two hours from Reunion Gap, smaller, nestled between mountains, curvy roads, and trees. Lots and lots of trees. The address Rebecca Nance had given her yesterday led Vanessa to a gray two-story with black shutters and a red door with a Christmas wreath on it. The house looked much newer than the other ones on that street, and Vanessa wondered if this was where Ethan grew up or if he'd purchased it for his mother later on. The answer was neither but it would take several minutes for Vanessa to understand that Ethan's mother didn't live here. In fact, she'd never lived at this address.

Rebecca Nance possessed grace, elegance, and the same eye and skin color as her son. There was a flawless beauty about her that said she would never look her age, and while she might prefer designer labels and pearls, she didn't need them.

She greeted Vanessa with a fierce hug, not a demure hand-shake and offered a heartfelt "I am so glad you've come into my son's life. So very glad." If the words did not say it, then the brightness in those dark eyes did. "Come, I have someone I want you to meet." Her voice dipped and she leaned close. "She's very special to Ethan and soon you'll see why. You'll also understand why it's important she give her blessing."

*Give her blessing? For what?* Since the phone conversation yesterday, Vanessa had attempted to piece together the mystery behind Rebecca Nance's words, but she'd ended with no success and a lot more questions. She followed Ethan's mother into a living room filled with a small Christmas tree, a welcoming fire, and scores of pictures frames—hanging on the walls, positioned on the mantel, shelves, the coffee table. The frames were different sizes, colors, shapes, with a large display situated on a table next to a middle-aged woman. Her style was simple: minimal makeup, dark hair streaked with gray, a gold locket dangling around her neck, a simple wedding band. The jeans and pink sweater were definitely not upscale and yet the woman made them look elegant.

"Vanessa, I'm Iris." Her blue eyes grew bright, filled with tears as she clasped Vanessa's hands. "How wonderful to meet you." Her gaze slid to Vanessa's belly. "A true blessing."

For a person who obsessed over the need to control situations, outcomes, and every variable in between, standing in a room with two strangers, clueless about what was about to unfold, was disconcerting. Vanessa wished she'd ignored Rebecca Nance's request to keep this trip from Ethan. She definitely should have told him all about it, maybe even asked him to accompany her to meet his mother and the mystery "Iris." But she hadn't and now all she could do was get through the visit and head back to Reunion Gap and Ethan.

"Please, sit." Iris released Vanessa's hands, motioned toward the floral couch. "I just baked banana bread this morning. Would you care for a slice with a cup of tea?"

Vanessa found her way to the couch and sank onto it. "No, thank you." She wasn't hungry, hadn't been since the phone call yesterday.

Rebecca Nance sat next to her on the couch, slender hands folded in her lap. "You must have so many questions, and I plan to answer all of them." A pause, a gentle smile. "We are truly delighted you've come into Ethan's life."

"Yes, he's such a wonderful boy." This from Iris whose eyes misted. "I do hope he can stop blaming himself for a past he couldn't control and find happiness at last."

*A past he couldn't control?* Vanessa sipped in tiny breaths, tried to remain calm. There were secrets here, ones that affected her and Ethan and their future. She could sense it in the looks the two women gave each other, in the tone of their voices when they spoke of Ethan. There wasn't enough information to piece anything together. Not yet. Vanessa turned to Rebecca Nance, held her gaze. "You said this trip might help him. That's why I agreed to come and why I didn't mention it to him. I don't like keeping secrets from Ethan and I plan to tell him as soon as I get back."

The expression on his mother's face did not look like a woman who was annoyed or displeased with what she'd just heard. In fact, she looked happy and her next words confirmed Vanessa's deductions. "You can't know how delighted I am to hear this. I can tell you and my son have a solid relationship built on trust and love." A sniff, a nod. "One can't ask for more than that."

"Indeed not." This from Iris, who sat back in her rocker, let out a sigh. "We have so much to tell you. Where do we even begin? Perhaps we should start with the way he was before, share how he helped so many people, and was a true joy to be around." She sniffed, pinched the bridge of her nose. "Or maybe we should concentrate on after, when he left a piece of himself in the grave with Darcy."

*Darcy?* "Darcy?"

Iris spoke. "Darcy. My daughter. Ethan's fiancée." She blinked, gripped the arms of the rocker, repeated. "Darcy."

*Dead fiancée*. Of all the reasons Ethan had kept his distance from relationships, Vanessa never considered this possibility. He *had* loved someone and she hadn't broken it off with him. No, she'd *died* on him. That was so much worse.

Rebecca Nance's voice drifted to her, filled with sorrow and pain. "I think we should start at the beginning." She drew in a breath, let it out and began to speak. "First, we are thankful you're here. Who knows how long or if my son would have told us about you and the baby? You see, Ethan's past hurt kept him from opening up and trying again. We never wanted that for him, and that's why we felt it was essential to invite you here." Pause and a cautious "We think you can help him get past that hurt."

Iris nodded, shared more. "Our hope is once you learn Ethan's real story, you can help him open up and find the life he deserves. The joy and happiness that should belong to him." A sad smile flitted across her face. "Whatever dreams he shared with my daughter have long since passed, but we believe he clings to them so he never has to risk getting hurt again. And if you didn't know about Darcy then you probably also don't know he visits me once every other month, sends Rebecca on trips, buys both of us things we don't want..."

"Tries to keep everyone happy." This from his mother who shook her head, dabbed her eyes with a tissue. "Everyone but himself. All the while insisting he *is* happy, that he does have joy in his life with his order, and his fancy cars and his penthouse...and the custom suits. He has *things*, Vanessa, and things don't make a person happy, not for long anyway. We're still the same person inside and when we realize that, we need to buy more things because we don't want to admit the emptiness. I should know because I spent a good part of my life attempting to make up for our lack of money and Ethan's lack of a father." Her voice cracked, wobbled as more truths spilled out. "I never realized what I was doing to him, not until a few years ago and by then it was too late. He'd built a wall so high around his feelings that I couldn't get near it. But you climbed over it, don't you see? Ethan let you in and now he just needs to see you'll care about him despite the pain inside, and the fact that he's not perfect. He needs to know you'll love him anyway." Pause and a soft "Won't you?"

Such a desperate plea from a mother who recognized her son's missteps. Vanessa realized she hadn't climbed any walls, at least not the ones to Ethan's heart. Those were protected by a dead fiancée and no one was getting past that. Maybe that had been his plan all along: he could care about Vanessa, grant her marginal entry into his life, but never engage in the full-on sharing like she'd done with her confession about Armand. Yes, he'd admitted a few deficiencies in his family dynamics: the absent father, the mother who gave him everything, even when they couldn't afford it...the job he'd taken to pay off his mother's debts and support her unwise choices.

But the rest? The big hole that had to do with relationships involving partners? He hadn't gotten near that, though he'd made comments. *I never understood the emotional attachments people form,* or *I can see how a person might get sidetracked and lose focus.* He'd made those comments when he'd been looking at her, those dark eyes bright, his voice low. Of course, she'd assumed he was referring to her. Why would she think anything else?

But that had been foolish wishing because it hadn't been about her at all. No, he'd never intended to go all-in and commit his heart and his life to her because he'd never let go of the fiancée he'd loved and lost.

"Please don't think poorly of him." Ethan's mother pulled Vanessa from thoughts of just how little she knew about the real

Ethan Nance. "My son means well, but he struggles to understand that a person must risk in order to fully know love and sometimes—" she cleared her throat "—*most* of the time, hurt is involved. Does that mean we should never risk? Absolutely not. I loved Ethan's father in a way I never thought possible, and yet I couldn't hold onto him. A child and a wife for a man like him weren't exciting enough, but that doesn't mean I regret loving him. I wouldn't have Ethan." A shrug, a sad "I wouldn't have memories of those few years of utter bliss when I was truly happy." Her eyes glistened, her lips pulled into a smile. "Perhaps you find this foolish, but I have *never* regretted loving that man and I tried to tell Ethan that many times over the years, but he either *cannot* or *will not* accept that."

It was Iris's turn to share. "Ethan lost my daughter in a tragic accident and the worst part was that he witnessed it." The woman's voice turned soft and melancholy as if she were reliving the events of that fatal day. "He'd been planning to propose...had tried to convince her not to ride her bicycle along the winding road that day...she didn't listen...she told him he worried too much..." Iris shared the rest of the tragic story, pausing to take a deep breath, clear her throat, and push past the pain. "Ethan changed that day. Gone was the young man who believed in dreams and forever. Gone was the hope of a family, a place to belong. Gone, and all that remained was guilt and blame and a vow to never open up to that kind of pain again."

Vanessa listened, tried to imagine Ethan planning a romantic proposal. She'd believed she could make him happy, show him love and how a person could share and trust. But it had all been a lie because she didn't know him. She placed a hand on her belly as if to protect her unborn child from the sadness that enveloped her.

The logical part of her brain took over as her heart shut down feelings for the man who had hidden his true self from her. She would have stood by him as he worked through his past, given him space and whatever he needed for a chance to share a life together. If only he'd been truthful, but he hadn't. No, he'd hidden his past, pretended she mattered and maybe she had—just not enough.

Vanessa sat through an hour of photo albums containing Darcy and Ethan. Rebecca flipped the pages of the first three albums, providing commentary with an occasional thought from Iris. "We want you to see his joy and how he could be that way again with you. It's buried in there; we know it is." Darcy was dark-haired, sun-kissed beautiful with a smile that lit up her face, while Ethan at seventeen was tanned, handsome, his expression lighthearted. There were so many pictures of happiness and love and meant-to-be... prom...baseball games, fishing, building a campfire, roasting marshmallows in the back yard...sitting on the hood of a car...holding hands...kissing...

"You can make him happy," Iris murmured. "The boy deserves to be happy."

Rebecca added her own spin. "He has to move on from the past. If he doesn't, how can the rest of us?"

"Look how happy he was? How filled with joy?" Darcy's mother sighed as she turned the page. "They had such plans...such dreams. Can you give him back his dreams?" She glanced up at Vanessa, eyes bright. "Please? Will you do it for us?"

Vanessa listened to tales of the man she'd believed could change her life, the one she'd trusted, the one she'd loved. But that person didn't exist. No, once again she'd chosen an impostor who said all the right words that meant nothing. Vanessa tried to ignore the mental images landing in her brain of Ethan and Darcy, failed. There were tears from the other two women, along with bits of laughter, and in the middle of it all, there was hope that this man they loved so much would finally get a second chance at love.

Vanessa would not tell them that whatever hope they had for her and Ethan had died the moment she discovered the secrets he'd kept from her. So many secrets. All she wanted to know now was who had told them about her and the baby. It wasn't Ethan and she couldn't imagine Daniel revealing such details. But who would have done it?

"Rebecca, you said a friend told you about me, but I can't imagine who that could be. Ethan's best friend is not the sharing type, so I'm perplexed. *Was* it Daniel Reese?" If it *were* Daniel, what would she do? Would she confront him, would she—

"No, dear, that wasn't the name." Rebecca reached out, patted her hand. "It was Mr. Alexander. Such a kind and caring man. I'm glad Ethan has a friend like him." Her dark eyes turned bright. "I could hear the culture in his voice, and the true kindness. I only wish there were more people in this world like him."

*Tate?* Tate had done this? "Was his name Tate?" Why would Tate divulge such details about her life? Why would he—

"No, dear, the man's name wasn't Tate. His name was Harrison. Harrison Alexander."

## 22

A bag of red tinsel rested on top of the ornaments Ethan ordered a few days ago. He'd also picked up several handmade ones from a local boutique: trees, candy canes, gingerbread men, stars. The plan was that he and Vanessa would decorate the tree tonight. Of course, he hadn't told her about the six-foot blue spruce he'd purchased at the local Christmas tree farm an hour ago, but she'd see it when she got home. When was the last time he'd decorated a Christmas tree? He was pretty sure it was high school, and he hadn't "celebrated" the holiday since losing Darcy.

This year would be different, and it was all because of Vanessa.

Everything was different because of her. Life was different in the very best way.

Tonight, they'd decorate the tree, listen to Bing Cosby sing "I'm Dreaming of a White Christmas," and kiss under the mistletoe he'd hung in the archway to the kitchen. The mistletoe idea sounded ridiculous and made him look like a lovesick fool. Actually, that behavior looked a lot like Daniel since he found

Meredith. Ethan knelt on the floor, tightened the screw on the base of the Christmas tree holder.

So what? Was it really so bad to want to be with someone? To think about them and wish they were beside you? Would it be the end of the world if he opened up and cared? If he loved someone? That possibility had never even been an option after he'd lost Darcy, but Vanessa had changed all of that and it had nothing to do with the baby. Of course, he absolutely wanted the baby, but he also wanted Vanessa.

She challenged him, matched his intelligence, intrigued, and perplexed, and definitely supercharged his emotions. He'd *never* met anyone like her, not even Darcy, who'd been a free spirit but *not* a freethinker.

He straightened, brushed off his jeans, thought of the Christmas present he planned to give her. Actually, there was more than one present. There was the bowl Daniel designed from maple and walnut, the one his best friend called a blend of simplicity and style. Ethan had also reached out to Meredith and asked her to design a special headband just for Vanessa. *I think violet would complement her eyes, and if we have a girl, maybe we could go with the mother-daughter set. What do you think?* That had been the most ridiculous question of all because Meredith hadn't been able to speak through the sniffs and tears and when she did, there was nothing but excitement, awe, and pure joy in her voice starting with *I always knew you and Vanessa were destined to be together* and ending with more sniffs and *I'm so happy for you.*

There was also the baby ornament he'd found in Nicki Price's boutique. It was a small porcelain teddy bear tucked in a crib with *Baby's First Christmas* and the date scrawled on it. Ethan smiled when he thought of the "debate" he and Vanessa would have over whether this was technically the baby's first Christmas. He saw both sides of it, and whichever position she took, he'd choose the opposite so he could enjoy her brain at work. The woman certainly possessed the most intriguing thought processes.

Of course, it didn't matter which side she took, because he planned to buy another *First Christmas* ornament next year. The more ornaments, the better, right? He sighed, shook his head. Was he becoming one of those Christmas lovers, the kind who decorated every room and listened to Christmas carols all day?

No. Well, not yet. But give him another year or two and once the baby came...

*Once the baby came...*

Life was good, full of hope and possibility. When Vanessa returned, he'd tell her just how happy he was she'd come into his life, and he'd show her, too, with a kiss under the mistletoe, the special ornaments they'd unwrap as they decorated the tree, the holiday music... And later still, as they made love by the Christmas tree, she'd know she truly owned his heart.

He only wished she hadn't picked this particular day to be so secretive. *I have to go somewhere. It will take most of the day, so don't expect me until late afternoon. Trust me,* she'd said. *I need to do this.*

What could he say to that? He had to trust her because relationships were built on trust and he understood that now. That's why he needed to tell her about Darcy and the home he had built for Darcy's mother and how he still visited the woman, reminisced, spent time with her. Ethan would share all of this with Vanessa because that's what relationships and *love* were all about.

And he loved Vanessa. Yes, he absolutely loved her and tonight, he'd tell her.

Three hours later, Ethan realized the perfect evening he'd planned down to the tiniest detail—candlelight dinner, shrimp, risotto with parmesan, mushrooms, and asparagus, with the "I love you" tucked deep in his chest—might not happen because he couldn't locate the woman who owned his heart.

Panic started in his gut, slithered to his chest as the text messages and phone calls went unanswered. Where was she? He refused to consider something had happened to her, but all of the positive thoughts he stuffed in his head could not stand up to the repeated beeps from her voicemail or the request to leave a message.

*Where the hell was she?*

Ethan punched in Meredith's number, got her voicemail. Next came Daniel, who didn't answer either. When this was over, they were all going to sit down and formulate a plan for emergency situations when a person went MIA. Okay, technically, Vanessa was *not* missing because she'd never given him an exact return time other than late afternoon. But she hadn't ignored his phone calls since the early days of their "relationship" when she'd been avoiding him because he didn't fit into her life—or she didn't think he did. Those days were long gone because she *knew* she belonged, knew *they* belonged together. Emotion took over, smothered his brain with the belief that if she weren't responding to his text messages and phone calls, something was very wrong. But until someone, *anyone*, answered their damn phone, all he could do was wait.

ETHAN JUMPED up from the couch when the car pulled into the driveway. He raced to the front door, flung it open and stepped onto the landing. Snow swirled around him, settled on his hair, his sweater and jeans, but he didn't notice. All he saw was the woman who'd stolen his logic and his heart. She was safe!

He hadn't taken a full breath in hours, not since his first call went to her voicemail. "Hey, I've been worried about you.

Where've you been?" What he wanted to say was *Why didn't you answer your phone? Did you count your missed calls? Why did you let hours elapse without contacting me? Do you have any idea how scared I was that something had happened to you?* But he'd wait until she was inside, after he'd kissed her and pulled her into his arms. *Then* he'd offer the suggestion about letting him know where she was and answering her phone. Vanessa was an independent woman and he admired that about her, but there was a point where a person needed to consider the *other* person in the relationship. And they *were* in a relationship, no doubt about it. This whole caring and sharing thing was foreign to him, but he'd do it for a chance with her. Hell, he'd do anything for a chance at a life with her. "Vanessa? Where were you?"

"We need to talk." She brushed past him, opened the door, and stepped inside.

The tone and the look said ticked-off and ready-to-unload—on him. How could she be upset with him when they'd been getting along so well? Talking, laughing, sharing. Happy. Not a word he'd ever particularly liked or used in everyday speech, but it fit. He and Vanessa were happy. But the woman he followed inside just now? The one who hadn't given a first *or* second look at the tree he bought today, hauled home, set up, and couldn't wait for her to see? He'd imagined her hugging him tight, soft body pressed against him, murmuring, *Thank you! Our first Christmas tree.* Yeah, not happening.

"All this time, you lied to me?" She shrugged out of her coat, tossed it on the couch and glared at him. "You let me believe you cared."

"What are you talking about?"

Disgust splashed her face, shot through her words. "I believed you, and you were just playing me."

"Vanessa." He moved toward her, stopped when she held up

both hands. "Okay, fine. I'll sit in the kitchen if you want. Just talk to me." Pause, followed by an almost desperate "Please?"

"I visited your mother today."

*"My mother?* Why? How?" The possibilities of how that happened and the reasons behind it landed in his gut like a greasy cheeseburger and fries.

"We had a very interesting conversation. She's beautiful, and she obviously loves you." Pause and a sharp "So does Iris."

Vanessa had met Iris? Then she knew about...

"Imagine my surprise when I learned you'd had a fiancée who died, and when you lost her, you swore you'd never let yourself get hurt like that again." A shake of her head, followed by a frown. "I opened up and shared parts of my life that were humiliating and painful, and you just sat there and said nothing."

Yes, he'd done that, but it wasn't that he didn't care about her or plan to tell her about Darcy—eventually. He *did* plan to share all of it. In fact, he'd intended to do it tonight, along with the other truth he'd been hiding; Vanessa owned his heart, *today and always.* But she wouldn't want to hear about that right now. He'd save it for when she forgave him...*if* she forgave him. "Please, let me explain."

"Explain? Sure, why don't you explain how you're in love with a woman I never knew about. Of course, I'm just a pregnancy source—a mistake—an afterthought that should never have happened."

*"You* are not a mistake." He moved toward her but she stepped back.

"Don't. No more smooth lines from the man full of fancy words and polish. I've heard enough. Your mother and Iris told me all about you, and how they believe you deserve a second chance." Laughter spilled from her lips: brittle, harsh, cold. "Apparently they think *I'm* the one to give you that second chance."

"You *are* the one who's made me believe in a second chance." Could she not see that? "It's all because of you, Vanessa."

"Stop, just stop." Her eyes grew bright, glistened with what might be anger or tears. "I sat for hours looking through photo albums, hearing how much you and Darcy loved each other and planned a future together. And then she died and you shut down, and you weren't the same person anymore. I heard it all, Ethan, and I'm the unlucky fool to have actually believed you cared."

"I do care. Vanessa, sit down. It's not good for you to be upset."

She sliced him a look that could have blown him across the room. "Don't worry about the baby. We'll be fine."

A burst of panic shot through him. "What does that mean?"

"It means you never wanted a baby and I never wanted a baby with you. And now we're both going to get exactly what we want."

Had her voice cracked just a bit, her lips wobbled? Was that pain buried somewhere beneath those perfect features? He'd never been able to tell what was going on in that brilliant head of hers. "I need to tell you the truth about Darcy."

"The truth doesn't matter now, does it, Ethan? It only mattered when I didn't know and you had a chance to tell me."

"I care about you, and I don't want to lose what we have." *I can't lose it and I can't lose you.*

"Don't want to lose it?" The snarl said she didn't like that comment. "You can't lose something you don't have. You're a sperm donor, that's all."

Ethan sucked in a breath, tried for calm, failed. How could she say that? *Why* would she say that? "You're going to look at me and say there's *nothing* between us but the baby?"

She squared her shoulders, bit out, "That's exactly what I'm saying."

Was she serious? Did she really *not* care about him at all? Ethan tried to see the truth but all he saw on her face was nothingness. "Darcy died when she was twenty-one. We were high school sweethearts, and yes, we planned a life together. I was going to propose the afternoon she died." He patted the front right pocket of his jeans. "I had the ring, I had the speech... I had it all prepared and I was waiting for her at our favorite spot...it's where we had our first kiss."

He didn't miss the reluctant curiosity inching across her face or the way her shoulders relaxed, as though she wanted to hear more. "Darcy was an exercise fanatic, rode her bike everywhere, even places she shouldn't, like on country roads in the late afternoon when the sun's low and you can't see what's beyond the next curve." His voice drifted as he recalled the details of that day. "We planned to meet at 4:30. I was already there, and when I spotted her coming around the bend... She saw me, I know she did because I still remember the big smile..."

He blinked hard, tried to destroy the vision of the car hitting Darcy, sending her over the guardrails. No use. "The driver who hit her had just gotten her license three months ago. She said the sun was in her eyes and she never saw Darcy." He cleared his throat, pushed past the sight of his almost fiancée lying at the bottom of the ravine. "I tried to get to her, but there were too many rocks, and no clear path. They didn't retrieve her body until several hours later. The coroner said she died instantly, but I don't really know if that's true or if he was trying to help me." He blew out a long sigh. "I suppose she could she have survived for a few minutes, but probably not."

"I'm very sorry."

"The town didn't blame me, but I blamed myself. If I hadn't been so stupidly romantic and insisted we meet at that place, she might still be alive. Or, if I'd nagged her about that bicycle and the dangers of it... The scenarios go on and on, all of them ending with me as the cause of her death. But the logical side of me understands there was no stopping Darcy's impulsive nature. She did what she wanted to do, and no amount of reasoning could stop her." He tossed out a harsh laugh. "Imagine me falling for someone who refuses to keep a schedule or set an alarm? I was different back then: trusting, light-hearted. Way too naïve. I believed in ridiculous words like *destiny, ever-after, forever.* And then she died and all those stupid beliefs died with her. All I could do was try to survive and vow to never put myself in that situation again."

"I see."

Ethan met her gaze, held it. "And then I met you."

She offered a tight smile. "Yes, and then you met me."

"I should have told you about Darcy sooner, and I'm sorry I didn't." He took a step toward her and this time she didn't back away or hold up her hands in protest. "I've never met anyone like you." Another step closer, then one more, until she was touching distance away. Ethan reached for her hands, raised them to his lips, kissed each finger. "We belong together, Vanessa. Forgive me and let's start again, all-in, no holding back?" She would not regret giving him a second chance and—

"I'm sorry, Ethan." She eased her hands away, stepped back. "It's too late. I can't trust you."

## 23

"Ethan Nance. I've been expecting you." Pause, followed by a curious, "Tell me, did your mother inform you of my phone call, or was it Vanessa Rodelle?" Another pause, a soft "The woman you impregnated?"

Ethan moved toward the man who was trying to destroy his chance at happiness, spat out, "You had no right to poke into my life."

"Right? You wish to speak to me about right?" The man squared his shoulders, eyed Ethan as though considering his plan of attack. "Do you believe you can threaten me, threaten what *belongs* to me and there will be no recourse?"

What was he talking about? Oh, of course. "This is about Meredith, isn't it? The great Harrison Alexander doesn't like that his daughter stood up to him, or that his son wants nothing to do with him."

"What I don't like—" the man's lips thinned, his voice turned cold "—is an outsider *intruding* upon family business. You had no right to advise, comment, or even think about my family. *My* family, not yours." The lips stretched, pulled into a smile. "Of course, you don't really have much of a family now, do you,

Ethan? No father, at least not one who's interested in being a father. You have a mother though she's not much of a guiding force or role model, and you've been supporting her since you were a teen. Then you have the woman who would have been your mother-in-law if your fiancée hadn't died on you. Bad bit of news about that. Sorry for your loss." There was absolutely no sympathy in his voice as he continued. "And now you have Vanessa Rodelle. Beautiful, intelligent, perfect for you. And she's even carrying your baby. But perfect doesn't win the game, not when I'm playing. I never forget a slight and you, Ethan Nance, have caused me a great annoyance, one I intend to squash."

"I'll destroy you, Alexander." Ethan clenched his fists as rage surged through him in ways he hadn't felt since Darcy's death.

"I accept the challenge. But remember, I don't follow rules made for ordinary men. I bend them, I break them, I do whatever's necessary to achieve my goal. You should know that." The silver gaze narrowed. "Let us not forget Oscar Reese and what happened to him. That was only a warm-up compared to what will happen to you if you continue to interfere in my life."

"You spent a good part of your life destroying people. Has it been worth it? Have you achieved your goal? Won the power and lost your family?"

"Do not mention my family again. They are *my* blood, *my* family, and if you had not intervened, the situation would be very different today."

"You mean the situation with Tate, don't you?" The flicker of pain that shot across the man's face said he'd hit the target. "Of course, it's always about Tate, isn't it? Meredith was only an avenue to get to him. Tate's the son whose affection and respect you want more than anything but can never quite seem to attain. What's your goal, Harrison? Working side-by-side with him in the business? Eating Christmas dinner, sharing a good scotch at the end of the night? Planning your next conquest with him right next to you?" Ethan laughed. "Your son is nothing like you. He's a man of honor, integrity, and character, and he won't let you destroy that or those he cares about…"

"Enough. When I'm finished with you, Vanessa Rodelle will despise you."

"I'm pretty sure she already does. Do you know you've taken my chance for happiness and the one thing I started to believe in again—hope—and you've made me desperate? Do you know what a desperate man does, Harrison?" When the man remained silent, Ethan offered up more truths. "A desperate man grows determined, and this desperate man will make sure you don't harm Tate, or Meredith, or Vanessa, or any of the Reeses…or the next unsuspecting victim who crosses your path."

Alexander laughed. "I welcome the challenge."

The man truly had no soul. "As do I. You've been warned." And with that, Ethan turned and left the Alexander mansion.

His next stop was Tate's office. If Ethan had any hope of protecting those he cared about, especially Vanessa, he needed Tate's help. Did Ethan want to spill the sad state of his personal life and how he'd created the disaster with Vanessa? Of course not, but Harrison Alexander was a menace who enjoyed destroying people's lives, and his eldest son was the only one who could stop him.

Ethan was usually the one behind the big desk, making decisions about situations and outcomes. Not this time. Tate listened, remained silent until Ethan finished telling him the whole story, including the part about Vanessa's visit to his hometown where she learned all about his dead fiancée from the two women who shared truths that should have come from him. "If I had been honest with Vanessa, then your father wouldn't have any leverage over me, but I waited. I swear I planned to tell her, but it wasn't soon enough." He dragged a hand over his face, let out a ragged sigh. "Good intentions don't matter. They only mattered *before* she found out. Now, she despises me."

Tate picked up a paperweight, turned it over, spoke in a quiet voice. "Yes, it would have been a lot easier, but you're not the first person to withhold vital information that lands on your chest. I get it, trust me, I do. We're so busy trying to protect ourselves that we don't see the landmines right in front of us."

"So, now what do I do?"

"Figure out a way to get Vanessa to trust you again. It will be a monumental task, but I think you can do it." Those silver eyes sparked, his voice shifted with determination. "I'll take care of my father."

VANESSA RUBBED her belly in a small, circular motion. Her pants were getting tighter and forget trying to get them zipped up. She'd planned to hunt for maternity clothes at Nicki Price's boutique, but she just didn't have the energy or the desire right now. How could her life have become unrecognizable in less than twenty-four hours? The hope she'd let into her heart had shriveled, replaced with sadness, disappointment, and misery. She'd finally trusted a man again and he'd betrayed her. Oh, he didn't think of it that way, but then why would he when she hadn't been the one who'd withheld vital information? No, she'd told him all about Armand and her pathetic and regrettable marriage.

And he'd said nothing about his own tragedy. Not. One. Word.

The opportunities had been there, many times, and yet he'd remained quiet. Until now. Because he'd been discovered? Because there was no way out of this twisted mess except to tell the truth? Who knew and yet he wanted her to trust him and vowed it would never happen again? Was that the truth? Or was it only the truth now that he'd been found out? If she agreed, would she live the rest of her life wondering what else he hadn't told her?

She could not go through that again, especially with Ethan. There'd been such a connection, like one she'd never known before. She'd *loved* him and he'd destroyed that, left her with pain and misery. Well, she would not make the mistake of letting him in or trusting him again.

When Vanessa returned from Ethan's yesterday—she no longer thought of it as home—Jennifer must have spotted the tragic expression on her face because she'd inquired *What's wrong? You don't look well.*

In less than five minutes, Vanessa spilled the entire tale of exactly how Ethan Nance broke her heart and her trust. For a woman who's known her own share of love and loss, Jennifer listened, offered comfort, a few tissues, and an encouraging smile. But she also asked the questions that, according to her, required answers before Vanessa could move forward with her life.

*Why would he park himself in Reunion Gap if he weren't committed to you and the baby?*

*Do you think he planned to tell you about the fiancée?*

*Do you really think he's the type of man who can be coerced into doing something he doesn't want to do?*

*Can you see a life without him in it?*

*Could you ever give him another chance?*

*Do you love him?*

*Well?*

*Do you love him?*

And the big one, the one that squeezed her chest. *Can you*

*picture him with someone else? In someone else's bed? Holding someone who isn't you?*

*Can you envision moving on in a life without Ethan?*

Vanessa wanted to lash out and insist she didn't want to hear or see that man again, didn't want him coming near her until the next prenatal visit. But there were too many questions with confusing answers so she settled for an answer that wasn't an answer at all. *I can't want to be with him and I can't open myself to trust or love him. I just can't.*

After a sleepless night that Vanessa blamed on her current state of mind and *not* the absence of Ethan's warm body next to hers, she dragged herself out of bed, showered, and made her way to breakfast.

"I was just coming to check on you. It's almost 11 o'clock." Jennifer set a cup of tea in front of her. "You shouldn't go this long without eating. How about eggs and toast with a side of strawberries?"

Vanessa forced a smile, shook her head. "I don't think I can manage that much right now. Maybe a bowl of oatmeal with a few blueberries?"

"Sure." Jennifer paused, her gaze homed in on Vanessa's belly. "You have to eat... For yourself and for the baby."

"I know. I will." Another forced smile and a soft "Thank you for being here for me."

Jennifer's voice filled with conviction, turned fierce. "I've been where you are and I'll do anything to help you."

## 24

E than had been summoned to what Tate called a Donovan intervention. *These people are not going to sit by and do nothing.* He'd patted Ethan on the back, laughed. *Take that as a good sign because if they didn't like you, they'd ignore you.*

*A Donovan intervention? I'm not sure I like the sound of that one.*

*You probably won't like what they have to say either, but whatever it is, will probably be true. I've been included in a few of these myself and sometimes I'm in the hot seat. You'll see. Just listen, smile, and try not to look annoyed even if you are... Scratch that, I mean, even when you are.*

The annoyance began eight minutes after Ethan walked into Rogan Donovan's kitchen. Small, compact, with a table that dwarfed the room. Rogan sat at the head of the table with his brother Luke beside him. And damn, if Daniel wasn't sitting next to Luke, beer bottle in his right hand. Interesting that his best friend had neglected to mention this meeting.

"Good to see you again, Ethan." Rogan stood, shook his hand, followed by Luke.

Daniel nodded and saluted him with his beer. Yeah, they were definitely going to have a talk later about how best friends stuck together and helped each other.

Luke Donovan, the one Meredith said was a reckless wanderer before he met his wife, pointed to the counter behind Ethan. "Help yourself to the booze. We've got high-end scotch thanks to our brother-in-law, whiskey, five types of beer in the fridge. Take your pick."

"Thanks." Now would not be the time to admit he'd given up drinking during Vanessa's pregnancy. That would make him look weak and foolish and—

"He's not drinking until the baby's born." This from Tate, who added, "I think that's a really noble gesture, especially from a scotch drinker."

And there it was…the disclosure that made him look like an idiot *and* a fool considering the woman he made that pledge for wanted nothing to do with him. "It seemed like the right thing to do at the time."

Luke rubbed his jaw, set his beer bottle on the table, and offered a proposal. "Yeah, but since you guys are on the outs, you could probably say you're taking a break… You know, like your relationship is right now?"

Luke Donovan might claim to be a reformed man, but he still had a lot of reckless inside him. "No, but thank you. Water's fine."

Rogan glared at his brother, leaned toward him, and said something in his ear that made Luke scowl. "Okay, okay, I was just offering a solution." He cut a glance at Ethan, shrugged. "Sorry, I was just trying to help. You looked like you needed a drink, maybe three."

Tate eyed Luke. "Not everybody solves problems with alcohol." He grabbed two bottles of water, handed one to Ethan. "Okay then, why don't we get started?"

"Hey, hey, hold on a second." Luke's blue gaze zeroed in on Tate's water bottle, shot to his face. "Is there something you're not telling us? You're drinking water... He's drinking water because his Baby Mama's pregnant..."

"Baby Mama? Really? Her name's Vanessa." Rogan shook his head, offered an apology. "My brother's still learning the finer points of politeness."

Luke shrugged. "Just trying to lighten the mood. It's not like we haven't all been there." He took a long pull on his beer, set the bottle on the table. "So, Tate, is there something you and Charlotte haven't told us? Are you adding a nursery to the Alexander mini-mansion?"

Tate Alexander might possess style and class, but the man had a look that could cut you five ways in less than a second. "No comment."

Most people would take that for what it was—*Don't want to talk about it and not going to talk about it*—but apparently not Luke Donovan. "No comment as in not true or no comment as in sound possibility but keeping it quiet for now. Or—"

"No comment as in no comment and none of your damn business."

Harrison Alexander might be an SOB who could intimidate and bully, but his son commanded serious respect. No doubt about it. But Ethan hadn't missed the split second of yearning and pain that splashed Tate's face before he answered. Was his wife trying to get pregnant and not having success? If so, had that made the man extra protective with this conversation? Ethan might be a guest, but he was not going to sit back and let the man who tried to help him get blindsided with comments like Luke had just made. "Isn't this meeting supposed to be about me and my less-than-stellar choices?"

Ethan unscrewed the bottle on his water, took a sip. "I mean, we all know I screwed up big time so can we just concentrate on me right now? Maybe each of you can offer a few pointers from experience, or just plain old common sense that could help? I've always been the problem solver and the fixer, at least for everyone else, and I'm not accustomed to asking for help." He blew out a long sigh, his gaze shifting to Daniel who stared at him, jaw twitching, lips flattened. "I don't do well with sharing personal information. I never wanted to look weak or vulnerable, but I guess I should have realized it only made me look human." Ethan forced out a laugh. "Maybe that's what I was trying to avoid...the looking human part."

"Good point." Rogan Donovan once again became the voice of reason and leader of the meeting. "I'm all for staying on track and trying to find a way to help dig you out of that hole you fell in and—"

"You mean the grave, don't you? The grave he dug for himself and could have crawled out from at any point if he'd bothered to ask for a hand." Daniel burned him with a look, followed it with harsh words. "Do you have any idea how much grief I'm catching from my wife right now? She's begun to wonder if you're untrustworthy and that's got her in a spin because she's the one who convinced Vanessa to take a chance on you."

"Take a chance on me?" Ethan stared at his best friend. "What am I? A prize at a carnival?"

That comment made Luke howl and damn if Rogan's lips didn't twitch.

Ethan cleared his throat, tried to take control of a situation that was about to land on him. "Can we discuss Meredith's concerns later. In private?"

Daniel eyed him a second too long, shrugged. "Sure, but why don't you tell everybody what's going on, how you plan to fix it, and why you think Vanessa should give you another chance?"

Ethan had never been good at sharing personal situations and

Daniel expected him to blurt it all out in front of these men? They'd want real answers too, not ones that said nothing and sounded like what he thought they wanted to hear. His gut told him they'd know the difference and call him on it. But what if he really *didn't* know what he planned to do, like now? What if he were mired so deep in a mess of his own making that he didn't know how or if he could dig his way out? "I screwed up, and for probably the first time in my life, I can't see a way out of it."

Daniel mumbled a curse, snorted. "I always told you that one day that brain of yours would get you into trouble and now it has."

One by one, the men shared their stories of how they'd almost lost the woman they loved, mostly through their own stubbornness and fear to open up and trust. And forgive. There were all sorts of situations—from secret identities, a fake marriage, bad blood, and mistrust to about every other situation that could wreck a relationship. The men insisted Ethan's current "issue" was no worse than what they'd been through, but it didn't feel that way to Ethan. No, to him it felt hopeless and unforgivable. Maybe because he wanted things to work with Vanessa in ways he'd never expected. Letting the emotions surface and rule over analytics was foreign, uncomfortable, and confusing.

Still, this group believed Ethan and Vanessa had a chance.

"Know what I think you need?" Luke Donovan smiled, said in a knowing voice, "You need to start sending Vanessa some of those I'll-love-you-forever cards my wife makes."

"I'm not so sure about that." Ethan had heard about the Annabelle Grace line. Even a relationship-phobic person like him had seen them. Gag-worthy, he'd once called them. He'd read a few, had even had the misfortune to be on the receiving end of one or two. He'd been so certain the whole concept was foolish and implausible, but that was before Vanessa. Now he understood and he'd send one of these cards every day if she'd consider giving him another chance.

"Luke's right. Women love those cards and Helena has partnered with my wife to create a whole new line." Rogan raised his hands, made air quotes with his index fingers. "They call it the 'feelings' line. Elizabeth is an artist, so she illustrates and Helena composes." He stopped short of an eye-roll, shrugged. "Women love them, and for us guys it's a sure way to get noticed, forgiven, *and* accept help for feelings that are difficult to get out. Do I particularly like what they say?" Another shrug, a shake of his head. "Not really, because I'm not that guy, but I do realize those words are necessary. My wife likes to hear me read them, so I do it because while she lives in my soul, she can't see *inside* my soul."

"Yeah, what Rogan just said." This from Luke, who grinned. "Helena says I inspire her and that's good enough for me. I like to steal a few of her lines and write a note…stick it on her pillow or next to her coffee cup… She thinks I'm a king."

Tate cleared his throat. "Okay then, let's agree on the cards. Buy a stack, add a few words of your own and start sending them."

"Yup… Start sending those suckers." Luke lifted his beer, saluted Ethan. "It could take six, seven, seventy-six. Maybe you'll buy enough to fund my kid's first year of college." The laugh said Ethan had his work cut out for him.

"I guess I can do the cards. Do they sell them in this town?" He could try the grocery store, but maybe he'd have to go online and—

"Nicki Price's place has them," Tate said. "I'll take you there."

"Thanks." Ethan glanced around the room. "What else can I do to fix this mess?"

Daniel was definitely annoyed about his wife's current state of unhappiness and his next words showed it. "You can start by burying the smooth talk and saying what you mean, not what you think she wants to hear." Pause and a firm, "That's a good start."

"Okay, I can do that."

"Get the touchy-feely cards, cut out the smooth-talk BS and —" Luke eyed the men at the table "—what else can the guy do? I guess the question is, what did we have to do because we've definitely all been there. How can we help this sorry guy earn another shot?"

The possibilities flowed around the table, most of them from previous experience. Some had worked, some required additional assistance.

*You send food, knowing you might not be invited to share it.*

*Flowers… Lots of flowers. What's her favorite?*

*Chocolates… Is she into dark chocolate or milk? Nuts? Almonds, hazelnuts, cashews?*

*Be patient.*

*Don't be a jerk.*

*Tons of cards.*

Daniel was the one who offered keen insight into what might actually help Ethan the most. "Each of us knows what touches us the most and how we can show just how sorry we are and how much we want that chance. For me, it was creating a line in Meredith's name, but more importantly, telling the whole world that I was Langston Turnings. For a guy who values his privacy, that was a big deal. That's what changed everything for me and while I didn't deserve it, Meredith gave me another chance. I vowed I would never keep anything from her again and I won't."

"Charlotte and I made the same deal about never withholding anything, no matter how small." Tate's voice grew quiet as if remembering less-than-happy times. "We had some rough days more than once. After we got through them, we promised each other we were never going there again."

"Agreed." Luke's usual teasing tone shifted, turned serious. "Helena and I never want a repeat of those times."

"We'll help you," Rogan said. "We'll talk to our wives and get their opinions. If they agree, they might help you. Women see situations we don't, especially when it has to do with relationships. Get them on your side and you'll have a shot."

"But if they detect BS or a smooth line, you're done." Daniel stared at him, his expression fierce. "You won't get another chance, trust me on that."

Ethan stared back, determined. "All I want is one chance. I don't intend to blow it."

## 25

Ethan was well aware of Harrison Alexander's exploits. When the man tried to destroy Daniel's father with blackmail, Ethan had made it his goal to learn everything he could about Harrison Alexander, especially the sinister parts. But there'd been nothing to prepare him for the man's presence or the vow that he'd ruin anyone who stood in the way of what he considered right and just.

But there *was* one person who could make the man re-think his treacheries. That person had just entered his father's library while Ethan remained in the hallway, the perfect spot to listen and not be seen. The plan was for Ethan to hold back a few minutes and wait for Tate to summon him.

Harrison's voice sifted from the library, happy, at ease. "Son, it's always so good to see you. Would you care for something to eat? I can have Cook prepare whatever you like."

"What I'd like is a few words with you."

"Of course." Pause and then "Would you care for something to drink?"

Tate's voice shifted to the hallway, cold, determined, fierce. "No, nothing to drink either."

"Well, if you change your mind, just say the word."

"Why is it that you can't call people by their names? That's Willa. She replaced Astrid."

"You mean the woman who left my employ to work in yours?" A sniff, a sharp "If it had been anyone but you, I would have blackballed her."

Tate ignored the comment. "I'm not here to discuss Astrid or Willa."

"I deduced as much. And since you aren't interested in a meal or a beverage, this must be about business. Am I correct?"

"Oh, it's business all right."

"Excellent." Excitement thrummed through Harrison's voice. "I've been following the restaurant project you're working on with Jameson Price and I have a few thoughts on—"

"This isn't about the restaurant. It's about Ethan Nance."

"Nance? I see that man your sister calls 'husband' has convinced you to intervene on behalf of his friend."

"Actually, Meredith doesn't know anything about this visit. I'm here because Ethan is *my* friend and I want you to leave him alone. You had no business getting involved with his personal affairs."

"Personal affairs?" The man laughed. "You mean making sure the woman who's carrying his child knows about the dead fiancée he conveniently neglected to mention? *To anyone?* I did the poor woman a favor. The man is nothing but a self-important, arrogant loser whose own father didn't care enough to stick around. Did you know he maintains a relationship with the dead fiancée's mother? Bought her a house, visits her on a regular basis, no doubt pretends the daughter is merely away and returning any moment." Another laugh, this one colder than the last. "And they say *I* engage in psychological manipulation."

"You just love having people investigated, don't you? Does it make you feel powerful? Do you like finding out how others have suffered?"

A snort. "It's called gaining an advantage."

"I call it manipulation and I'm done having you manipulate people I care about. Stay away from Vanessa and Ethan and anyone associated with them."

"Anyone? *You're* associated with them." Pause, followed by a sly "Does that include you as well?"

"I'm the exception, but I won't be if you can't respect the rules."

"Rules? *Rules?* I make the rules, Tate, don't you realize that? Nobody tries to disrupt my life, ruin my relationship with my children, and threaten me without retaliation. That man did all three. Surely you knew I would strike back."

"No, I suppose I didn't because I gave you a chance to honor your word and once again, you proved you couldn't be trusted, even with an obvious and indisputable request. Did I not say you were to stop meddling in Meredith and Daniel's lives? Did I have to include everyone associated with them?"

"That's nonsense and soon enough, you'll realize what we can achieve together."

Tate ignored the comment, provided his own challenge. "You *will* apologize to Ethan and you'll give your word, even though it might not be worth much, that you'll leave him alone. If I hear your name attached to *anything* pertaining to Ethan, you're done. No more warnings, no more meetings. I'll cut you out of my life, and I'll never see you again."

Silence. And then, "Why can't you see the inherent weakness in most people? They lack the spine to commit to what needs to be done, no matter how difficult or distasteful. The strong recognize the necessity and accept the challenge, while the weak run and cry outrage as they're trampled upon. Remember, the powerful take, the weak relent. Do not let me think you've become weak."

This time it was Tate who laughed and his father must have recognized the cold dismissiveness in that laugh because his next words were not so demanding. "All I want is to spend time with you, son—in business, and otherwise. Have I not accepted the Donovan girl?"

"The Donovan girl is my *wife*, and her name is Charlotte."

"Yes, that's what I said. And now your sister's gone and picked up a stray and we must accept that he'll infiltrate the Alexander bloodline as well. Who's next? Are we to allow all of them in?"

"I'm going to ignore those comments. I want you to leave Ethan Nance alone, *and* I want you to apologize to him."

"Apologize? And what about him? Do you think it's acceptable to deceive the woman he supposedly loves, the one carrying his child, and let her believe he's someone he's not? And what of the deep, dark secrets he never bothered to share? Should he hide those from her as well?"

"This from a man with more secrets than the whole town combined."

*"I am your father.* While you may not agree with me, I did everything for you and because of you."

Another laugh, this one colder, more brutal than the last. "You almost destroyed me and you left scars on all of us. Not the kind you can see, but the ones deep down in our souls. Me, Meredith, Neal. You taught us that we were never good enough, relationships were worthless, love and respect for your partner didn't exist. Meredith and I figured out those were lies, but Neal still believes them. And *that's* why he turns from one woman to the next. It's because of you, *Dad*…that's the legacy you left us. And now you have one small opportunity to make it right with

Ethan Nance and if you value what I think about you, you will leave that man and everyone associated with him alone."

Long pause, followed by a sigh. "If I do this, do I have a chance with you?"

Tate didn't answer for several seconds, and when he responded, it wasn't really an answer at all. "If you don't do it, you'll have no chance."

Harrison offered a grudging "Very well. I'll pen a note by the end of the week."

"Not necessary. You can tell him in person. Ethan? You can come in now."

Ethan stepped from the hallway into the library, oblivious to the elaborate room: the glossy wood finish, the floor-to-ceiling bookshelves, the artwork. If the library belonged to someone else, he would have appreciated the fine wood, the crystal, the art. But it belonged to a cruel and heartless man and that changed everything. All he saw in the center of the room was the man who'd destroyed his chance for happiness and love: Harrison Alexander.

"You..." Ethan's nemesis stared at him, the expression on his tanned face one of disbelief and fury. "You..."

Tate squared his shoulders, spoke in a voice that left no doubt who held the real power between the two Alexanders. "Ethan heard the entire conversation. Every last word. Now about that apology..."

ETHAN KNEW it was only a matter of time before his mother reached out to him. She actually made it three whole days, a remarkable feat for an impatient person like Rebecca Nance.

"Ethan, hello." The lilt in her voice said *happy*. "How are you?"

No doubt she believed he'd say something like *Wonderful… Never been better… Planning our future… One big happy family…* His mother had never been one to find problems just below the surface. She preferred to dwell on what she called "positive" moments. He could gloss over the truth and she'd probably accept that, but he was tired of pretending everything in his world was right, that he didn't want anything else, couldn't anticipate or imagine a different life. He wasn't going to do that any longer because he *could* imagine a different life, a better life, and he'd even experienced it for a short time—until he destroyed it. "I've had better days. How are you?"

"How should a grandmother-to be-feel? I'm absolutely ecstatic and Vanessa is delightful. What a gem." Her voice dipped, switched to intimate. "I'll bet you were surprised she came to see me, weren't you? I'm certain she told you all about the visit. Iris and I approve 1000 percent." Pause and a soft "We didn't ask but is there going to be a wedding? Of course, I know it's not necessary, but I was merely curious."

*A wedding?* Doubtful. For years, he'd been the one running from that possibility, laughing at the nonsense of such a union. But that was before Vanessa, before he discovered what being with a woman like her meant, what sharing could offer if you allowed yourself. Yup, and he'd annihilated every last bit of it. Ethan cleared his throat, forced out the truth. "I don't think so."

There was the tiniest hesitation that said "disappointed" but his mother buried it with her next words. "Vanessa said you don't plan to find out the sex of the baby. Now that surprised me since you're such a planner." A sigh and then "This is so exciting. Do you think I might visit you in Reunion Gap? I'd love to organize a shower or… whatever…"

"Mom, there's something you need to know."

"Ethan? Is something wrong?"

Now there was a question. "Everything. Every damn thing is

wrong." And then he proceeded to tell her exactly what that meant. He finished the sad story that had become his life, waited for his mother to boost him up with comments like *Everything will be fine,* and *She'll come around.* Even *You'll figure it out.* But she didn't, not this time. Instead, she spoke the words he wished she'd said years ago.

"I'm sorry I raised you to think your choices were always correct and that you didn't need to answer to anyone. I was determined to make up for your father's absence and vowed you'd never want for anything, even when I couldn't afford it. I didn't see that what you really needed from me was guidance and strength, not fancy clothes and summer camps." She sniffed, let out a soft sigh. "I should have told you the truth about so many things, and I should not have let you take responsibility for my poor choices. You were a child and yet you stepped in and got a job to help pay our debts. It wasn't right, but I didn't stop you."

"Mom, it's okay." Ethan rubbed his temples, tried to block out the painful memories of his past.

"No, it's not and for that I am truly sorry. Vanessa is a good person and I believe she loves you, but creating this persona who never makes a misstep? Hiding in a past she knows nothing about? That would be difficult to forgive, and I hope she can. Still, no matter what happens between the two of you, I'll be here for you: to listen if you want to talk, to support you as I should have so long ago."

*This* was his mother speaking? He couldn't ever remember a conversation where she'd shared so much and spoken with such candor. "Thank you" was all he could manage.

"The greatest gift I can give you is to tell you to be yourself, and stop trying to save everyone, especially me and Iris. We only want you to be happy, whatever that means for you. I love you,

Ethan. I am so sorry about all of this, but mostly I'm sorry for my part in it."

The shift in his relationship with his mother took place that day, and while his life was currently more messed up than it had ever been, there was an odd relief and a weightlessness since their conversation. Did he know what his life would look like in the coming days, weeks, years? *Absolutely not.* Did he hope Vanessa would be a part of it in a way that was so much more than just the mother of their child? *Absolutely.* Did he think it would happen? Now there was a question with an answer he didn't have.

# 26

---

The bouquet of red roses arrived at the Peace & Harmony Inn five days after Vanessa's fallout with Ethan. Tucked inside was a note. *I'm sorry. Love, Ethan.*

Vanessa should toss them in the trash, but they were too beautiful to discard. And the note? She should throw that away as well. What did words from a liar mean anyway? Nothing. She found a vase in Jennifer's kitchen, filled it with water and tucked the note in her pocket. She might be able to make an excuse for deciding not to discard the roses, but saving the note? That action meant something but her brain refused to acknowledge or play out the possibilities.

Red roses symbolized love. *Love.* Of course, Ethan knew that, just as he knew she did as well. He could say he loved her, write the words, and make promises, but was that the truth? Even if it were, love without trust couldn't last and Vanessa didn't trust him.

Could she ever trust him again?

On day two, he sent her two African violets, a deep purple one and a pale pink. Rich, dark-leaved, and perfectly formed.

There was another note attached to the second violet. *I've found that African violets require commitment and care and given both will never disappoint. Enjoy their perfect beauty. Love, Ethan.*

He may as well have said *I won't disappoint… I can be counted on… You can trust me and we can rebuild this relationship…* Symbolism at its best, meant for her aching heart. Vanessa placed the violets in a sunny window in the sitting room, settled in a chair and spent the next few hours staring at them, wondering about the man who'd sent them.

Two cards arrived a few hours later and she recognized the Annabelle Grace line. She'd been curious about what sort of person would write these when she learned Helena Donovan lived in Reunion Gap, and that made her even more curious. She studied the front: a single holly branch covered in red berries, dusted with snow. Beautiful, simplistic, so touching. Vanessa turned the card over, spotted the Annabelle Grace logo, along with *Illustrations by Elizabeth Donovan* and a one-line blurb that read *Love notes that touch the soul, embrace the heart.* She'd never pictured Ethan as a man who would send one of these cards though she could imagine him on the receiving end of several. Vanessa opened the card, read the *You are my one and only* sentiment that marked this particular line. At the end of the card, Ethan had written his own note. *I will always be thankful for the day you walked into my life. Love, Ethan.*

The second card arrived later that day and was filled with words of love and hope. But what she homed in on was the handwritten part after. *You are the most important person in my world. I hope you will find it in your heart to forgive me. Love, Ethan.* The Belgian chocolates came the next morning with the most beautiful orchid she'd ever seen.

"Wow, this is gorgeous." Jennifer leaned closer, studied the flowers. "I've never seen one quite this shade of pink."

Vanessa fingered a petal, thought about how much Ethan loved orchids. "It is stellar, isn't it?"

"Indeed, and the orchid isn't the only thing that's stellar." Jennifer smiled, slid her a knowing look. "I'm beginning to think there's a whole other side to Ethan Nance and you're going to witness it—in an up-close and very personal way."

Vanessa tried to fight the heat creeping from her neck to her cheeks. *Up close and personal?* It certainly felt that way. "He manipulates words for a living, so there is that to consider." Who was she trying to convince, Jennifer or herself?

"True, but nothing about his approach or the gifts feels contrived, and I'm a big skeptic. I think I'd sense it."

And that was the problem. Ethan Nance was so skilled in his delivery that he could make a nonbeliever trust him. Vanessa spent the rest of the evening studying the cards along with the handwritten notes, staring at the orchid, eating Belgian chocolates, and trying to figure out the man who continued to confuse her.

The card arrived the next morning with a fancy box containing ten dark chocolate almonds. She recognized Elizabeth Donovan's illustrations on the front of the card and expected to find Helena Donovan's sentiments inside. But when she opened the card, it was Ethan's bold handwriting that stood out.

*Dear Vanessa:*

*I have never been much for sharing and have spent most of my life solving other people's problems while ignoring my own. (Why would I attempt to solve my problems when I refused to admit I had any??) It's easy to look at life and expectations when you shut down possibility and hope. What is hope anyway? I'll tell you what it's not. It's not moving through your days as though you don't want to experience anything different... anything bordering on uncertainty.*

*You, Vanessa Rodelle, threatened my logic, my thoughts, my*

*certainty that I knew what I wanted and how I planned to live.*
*I had a chance for happiness, but fear kept me from grasping*
*it.*

*Fear I would be rejected, fear I would not be loved, fear I*
*would be too open and vulnerable. I couldn't let that happen,*
*could I? Yet I never stopped to realize that opening up to you*
*would bring freedom, happiness, love.*

*I am truly sorry that I didn't trust you enough to share my life*
*—my whole life—with you. I want us: me, you, the baby, and I*
*will never stop trying to earn your forgiveness or a second*
*chance. Love, Ethan*

VANESSA HAD NEVER DEVELOPED a group of friends, not real
ones she could talk to and certainly not as an adult. After the
disaster with Armand, she shut down, believed she could survive
on her own, rely on no one but herself. Life would be consistent,
steady, calm.

But what about the joy, the possibilities, the opportunity to
care...to mean something to someone and have someone mean
something to you? Friends included. Since arriving in Reunion
Gap, Vanessa was learning how much friendships and potential
friendships *did* matter, that people cared about her, not because
she had a high-powered job, contacts with industry profession-
als...none of that. They cared about her for herself, in spite of or
maybe *because of* the mess of her current situation.

Before coming to this small town, she would have been
mortified, definitely not happy to hear that others had been
discussing her personal life. Everything seemed to change when
she arrived in Reunion Gap. People reached out, asked questions,
expressed interest and concern. Real, not fabricated polite
niceties that had to be gotten through to get to the next part of the

conversation—the one that usually pertained to a deal or a situation.

Nine days after the fallout, Vanessa sat in the sitting room of the bed-and-breakfast, clutching Ethan's handwritten note against her belly. There was no use pretending she hadn't begun to look forward to the daily and sometimes twice-daily gifts, especially the notes and cards. This last one had touched her in ways she hadn't anticipated, stirred all sorts of emotions, some confusing, not all of them welcome.

Ethan had revealed so much about himself these last several days, and none of it had to do with his past or his background. No, it had to do with what lived deep inside his soul, heartfelt sharing of what mattered to him, the life he wanted—with her. He was no longer the aloof, arrogant know-it-all who never showed emotion. Instead, he let her see the real Ethan Nance: the one who cared, who bled, who was afraid and uncertain. Oh, but that man sounded so appealing, but what if he shut down again, refused to share? She couldn't give him another chance until she knew he'd always be honest with her. No matter what.

But how did a person ever really know?

This was the dilemma she'd been trying to analyze when Jennifer appeared in the doorway. "You have visitors."

"I do?" Her first thought was Ethan, but "visitors" implied more than one person. So, probably not. Vanessa didn't have time to consider who it might be when laughter spun through the hallway, accompanied by chatter. Seconds later, Meredith appeared, followed by Charlotte Alexander and Elizabeth and Helena Donovan.

"Hello, there," Charlotte said, sliding into a chair. "Happy almost Christmas."

"Thank you." Oh, she'd had such hopes and plans for a real Christmas this year, and then...

Meredith reached out, laid a hand on her arm. "We've been

waiting and following this saga, and we figured it's time for us to talk." Helena and Elizabeth sat on the couch, turned toward Vanessa, their smiles encouraging.

"Talk? I assume I'm the subject?"

Charlotte laughed. "Yes, you are. So is that handsome man of yours." Big sigh and a frustrated "We've been pestering our husbands for information, but you know how men are. They give you the abridged version but not the details…the ones we want."

"The details are what really matter, right?" Meredith made a face. "Men just deal in broad brushstrokes. 'They're working on it.' 'It's a process.' And 'Too soon to tell.' But women? We want it all, including the visuals. Men are just different when it comes to that stuff."

"True." Elizabeth lifted a delicate shoulder, shrugged. "But they know what we need and while I don't expect Rogan to write sonnets, he gets the important things."

A nod from Helena. "Same with Luke, even if he does 'borrow' a few of the lines from my cards. I don't care because it says he's taken the time and has the desire to tell me those things. And when he reads them out loud… Well, there's nothing quite like hearing those words from the person you love." Her voice gentled and she held Vanessa's gaze. "Ethan contacted me a few days ago to ask if he could buy a box of my cards. He handpicked them and also bought a few that were blank inside. I give the man credit because not many people would choose to add their own words when they can opt for pre-printed ones."

Vanessa clutched the card he'd written close to her belly. "Yes, he's been sending cards and yesterday he sent this one." She held up the card with the poinsettia flower on the front and the handwritten words inside. "It's a beautiful card."

"Sure is, and I'll bet you're not just talking about the flower." Charlotte homed in on the card. "Nope, the way you're hanging on to that thing, I'm guessing there are some pretty powerful words in there."

"Words are powerful, but sometimes they're just words." Vanessa wanted to believe what he'd written, wanted it so much and yet doubt still lived in her heart.

"True, but at some point, you're either going to take a leap and trust or you'll never trust again." Charlotte frowned, bit her bottom lip. "I know all about creating train wrecks and blowing up relationships, especially the only one that ever mattered to me. Tate did the same and I guess you have to decide if you want to get through it, too. It really is your choice because from what I can piece together, your guy might have started out sitting on the sidelines, closed off and closed up, but he's definitely all-in now and it has nothing to do with the baby."

Helena sighed, added, "I hear he bought a baby's first Christmas ornament. How sweet is that?"

It was Meredith's turn to sigh her approval. "I wasn't happy with the man for holding back, but I have to agree with Helena. He definitely wants a relationship with you, Vanessa, and I'm not talking about friendship. Do you know he asked me to fill out a questionnaire about you? There were all sorts of questions ranging from your favorite brand of chocolate to your shoe size, and if you favored a single or double strand of pearls?" Her blue eyes turned bright, her voice soft. "Don't give up on him. Can't you find a way to forgive and learn to trust him again?"

"There are moments when I want to...when I'm desperate to believe him, but then I think of the pain and how much he hurt me. I don't know if I could go through that again."

"Whenever we open ourselves to love or caring, we're bound to risk getting hurt." Jennifer stood in the doorway, hands clasped against her middle. "But what if you can get past it? What if you find a way to trust and open your heart? Imagine what that could be like? I'd call it close to Heaven."

"Paradise on earth," Meredith said with a faint smile. "Definitely."

Charlotte pointed to the card in Vanessa's hand. "Love is scary and messy but so worth the risk. We're all here for you, just a phone call away. Please remember that." She paused, said in a quiet voice filled with emotion, "Even the strongest and best relationships go through rocky times. It's all about how we handle it; do we fall apart, accuse, distance? Or do we talk it out, accept our differences, and try to find common ground? That's where real love comes in."

Elizabeth spoke next. "I never thought Rogan and I would get past our hurts. I lied to him and when he found out, I was sure I'd lost him. Actually, I *had* lost him...*and* I was pregnant. I waited for him to forgive me and when he didn't, I left town. And then, thanks to Tate, Rogan opened his eyes and tracked me down. We've been solid and inseparable ever since."

There were more stories with more details. As Vanessa listened to these women, she realized their experiences were as pain-filled and sad as hers. But the path to another chance was all about forgiveness, trust, and moving forward. And love. Lots of love. Vanessa placed Ethan's card in her lap, cleared her throat and glanced at the women who'd offered their friendship and support. "I'd like to thank all of you for coming tonight and sharing your stories. I've always been a private person, and this whole opening up and sharing is all new to me. But I'll get the hang of it, I promise I will." She cleared her throat again. "Thank you for your support, your kindness, but most of all, thank you for your friendship."

Jennifer stepped forward, swiped at her eyes, and said, "Now that Vanessa knows we've got her back, who wants sugar cookies and hot chocolate?"

## 27

Vanessa might tell herself she wasn't becoming obsessed with Ethan's cards and gifts, especially the handwritten notes, but that wasn't true. She'd found herself peeking out of the window this morning for special deliveries and checking her watch at least every twenty minutes. Ugh, what was she doing?

It didn't help that her new friends had opinions on what was happening and those opinions all centered on Ethan's declaration of love for her and his willingness to do anything for another chance. Helena called the "gifts" romantic and swoon-worthy, while Meredith insisted they were a prequel to a ring. Charlotte labeled them billboard-size confessions of love and commitment.

When lunchtime came and went with nothing from Ethan, Vanessa dug into work. However, it was difficult to get excited about the prospect of pitching to a new client when her whole life was a jumble of confusion. Still, she dove in, pretended she wasn't interested in the time of day or the possibility of something from Ethan.

By mid-afternoon, she couldn't pretend any longer. Why hadn't he sent her a note or a card? Was something wrong? Had someone told him there'd been a get-together at the Peace & Harmony Inn last night and he'd been the topic of conversation? He might be willing to open up, but she doubted he wanted the whole town to know his personal life. *That* was a huge stretch and maybe they'd pushed him too far. Maybe he'd decided this personal sharing business was a little too personal. She understood what that was like because she was still getting used to the open discussions and bold commentary from her new circle of friends.

Last night had certainly been an eye-opener in the lesson about relationships. She'd never thought much about it, had assumed people either clicked or they didn't. What she hadn't known and should have seen was that even the most perfect couples needed to work at being a couple. When they disagreed or couldn't understand the other's point of view, they worked through it because they loved each other. And they treated each other with respect and never let them forget they were the most important person walking this earth.

Did Ethan really feel that way about her? Did she feel that way about him? She cared about the man and pretending otherwise would be foolish. What she'd learned last night was that love was strong and precious, and mistakes and misunderstandings without forgiveness could destroy even the best and truest love.

At 4:05 p.m. a package arrived from Ethan containing body creams, soaps, scrubs, and a candle, all in her favorite scents: hyacinth and lavender. Tucked in the box were two envelopes, marked *one* and *two*. Vanessa opened the first envelope, slid out the card. The basic pencil sketch of a Christmas tree with presents looked more like a grade schooler's attempts and definitely not Elizabeth Donovan's artistic illustrations. When she opened the card, the first line told her who'd drawn the tree.

*Dear Vanessa:*

*I thought I would humor you with my artistic abilities—or perhaps I should say, my lack of artistic abilities. I was thinking about your laugh, the richness of it and the way it makes your eyes sparkle. I plan to picture you opening this card so I can "hear" that laugh.*

*I've been thinking a lot about hope. I've detested that word for years because to me it meant giving up or giving in to someone else. Hope on its own felt futile. Why would I give my power to that when I could create and control my own destiny?*

*But lately, I see hope as something quite different. Hope means possibility and opportunity and a chance to live.*

*I think of hope every day when I think of you.*

*I hope you will give me an opportunity to show you how good we can be.*

*I hope we will share a life together.*

*I hope you will forgive me.*

*I hope…*

*Love,*

*Ethan.*

Vanessa set the card aside, opened the second envelope, which contained a single photograph and a handwritten note.

*I've enclosed a photograph I took yesterday. It's the tree I bought at the Christmas tree farm the morning you visited my mother. I'd hoped we could decorate it together and I bought ornaments for us, for the baby, for our family. I hadn't decorated a tree since high school and I almost tossed this one out, but I couldn't do it because that damn hope wouldn't let me.*

*Instead, I decorated it, wrapped gifts for you and the baby and set them under the tree. Note, the dog in the photo is Winston; he belongs to Tate and Charlotte. Dogs are great company and I swear they know what you're saying and they absolutely know what you're thinking. Who cares about a little dog hair? After all, there's always a lint brush.*

*If you're free and want to listen to a little Johnny Mathis, or Neil Diamond—Oliver told me Neil was one of your favorites—I've got both. I'm thinking about making chicken risotto with broccoli because I remember how much you loved it. No pressure to stop by... If you don't, I'll send a care package to the bed-and-breakfast tomorrow. But if you do have an interest or the desire to stop by to see the tree and enjoy dinner, I'll be waiting. And hoping.*

*Love, Ethan.*

Vanessa studied the photograph: Winston the dog, the Christmas tree, the multicolored lights, red garland, the tinsel, balls and ornaments... She squinted, spotted *Baby's First Christmas* and then another... More squinting. Was that an ornament with *Our First Home* and the date at the top? She couldn't tell. And the presents under the tree? Goodness, there were so many of them, all different sizes and shapes.

*Oh, Ethan.*

She pressed the photograph against her heart, bent her head and let the tears come.

≈

ETHAN STRETCHED out on the couch, arms crossed behind his head, eyes closed, listening to Johnny Mathis sing "I'll Be Home for Christmas." The aroma of the chicken-broccoli-risotto dish reached him, reminding him his guest was a no-show. Why had he thought she'd actually come? Because she loved the risotto dish? Yeah, she might, but not enough to forgive him for his actions and stupidity.

Maybe she really wasn't going to forgive him. Ever. No, he couldn't let that possibility saturate his brain, not when he'd finally begun to believe in hope. Hope carried people through the difficult times, gave them strength to believe their lives would improve and possibility still existed.

He let out a sigh, opened his eyes and reached for the book on baby names. Today he felt like perusing girl's names. Catherine, Cecilia, Colette, Danica. What about Daniela? Would Vanessa like that? Or Elissa, Emma, Gabrielle? Ethan had made it to the *M*'s when the doorbell rang.

*Vanessa?* It was one thing to dream about her in this house, and another to invite her, but to possibly have her standing on the other side of the door? Ethan sprang from the couch, smoothed both hands over his hair, and adjusted his sweater. In less than eight seconds he'd open the door and be ecstatic or extremely disappointed. *Please, let it be Vanessa.* He placed his hand on the doorknob, opened the door.

And there she stood: beautiful, hesitant, serious.

"Is the dinner invitation still open?"

"Of course." *You can have anything you want...risotto, dark chocolate...me.* He pushed that last thought from his brain, held the door for her as her hyacinth-lavender scent drifted toward him. Oh, how he'd missed her.

Vanessa stepped inside, shrugged out of her coat, and handed it to him. "So, chicken and broccoli risotto?"

"And not just two servings." He worked up a smile. "More like twenty servings, definitely enough to feed half the street. Are you hungry?" His gaze slid to her belly, settled on the tiny bump beneath the red sweater. *Their baby.*

"I'm definitely hungry for that dish." She cleared her throat, shifted her gaze to the Christmas tree. "Wow." Vanessa moved toward the twinkling tree with the presents stacked underneath. "This is so beautiful." She inched closer, located the first baby Christmas ornament—a teddy bear tucked in a crib. "I love it," she murmured.

Ethan watched as she made her way around the tree, leaning

in close, touching a branch, tracing garland, studying the ornaments. "You did all of this?" She turned to face him, hazel eyes bright.

He nodded. "It was a process. I think I might have overdone it with the garland—" he laughed, pointed to the layers of red covering the tree "—but then I thought, can you ever have too much of the stuff? It just seemed to flow, so I kept adding more. I measured the longitudinal distance between the branches, but of course, the branches weren't equal distance from each other...so..." Ethan clamped his mouth shut before he admitted to drawing the tree to scale and calculating the amount necessary, along with the proper placement of the garland, to create a symmetrical effect. He sounded like an idiot and he should just shut his mouth, but it had been too long since he'd stood next to this woman, and he was desperate to keep her here.

Those full lips he'd tasted so many times pulled into a smile. "I think it's just perfect." She glanced at the presents beneath the tree. "Did you wrap all of these?"

A shrug. "Once you figure out a system, it goes pretty fast."

"I'm not so sure about that..." She bent toward a square box wrapped in red foil candy cane print. *"To our baby. Love Mom and Dad."* She ran a finger over the tag. "Mom and Dad. Sounds strange, doesn't it?"

"Truth?"

Vanessa straightened, turned to him, her expression serious. "Always."

*Truth* was a damn stupid word to use, considering their situation. "I kind of like it. I mean, once I got used to hearing it in reference to myself." He forced a laugh, offered another truth. "Though I'm not sure how much I'm going to like it sixteen years from now when we're dealing with teenagers. I hear they don't become normal again until nineteen." Ethan rubbed his jaw, considered the validity of his statement. "You think that's true?"

Her lips twitched. "Guess we'll find out."

"Do you think we'll make it?"

She blinked. "I certainly hope so."

*Wait.* Was she talking about the teenage years, or was she talking about *them*? Ethan replayed the last few sentences, the tone, the nuance, but he had no idea what she meant. It could be either one or it could be both, or—

"Ethan?"

"Yes?" But maybe it was only—

She smiled, said in a gentle tone, "Thank you for the cards and the gifts."

It was one thing to open your heart on a piece of paper or inside a notecard, but quite another to stand face-to-face so the woman you loved could get a firsthand glimpse of just how desperate you'd become. But desperation could drive a man to do just about anything, and that's where Ethan was right now. "You're welcome." If he were going to sacrifice his pride, then he planned to go all-in. "I was definitely outside of my comfort zone."

The smile inched wider. "No doubt." She took a step toward him. "My favorites were the handwritten notes. Very poetic for a man of numbers and spreadsheets."

He spotted the teasing tone, the sparkle in her eyes. If he could keep her relaxed and engaged, she could tease him all she wanted. "I considered rhyming verses, but I never made it past 'My heart is blue without you.'" She actually laughed at that one, which encouraged him to say more. "I spent three hours on the first note. Do you know how many business deals I could have analyzed in that amount of time? It was painful but I forged ahead, determined to get those feelings out no matter what." Ethan raised a brow, lowered his voice, "I haven't spent so much time handwriting *anything* since grade school." He lifted his hand, stretched his fingers. "I now understand all about cramped fingers."

Her face lit up as she offered him a brilliant smile. "Well, know your efforts were appreciated. Thank you."

"For that smile, I'd be willing to suffer the occasional cramped finger."

She shook her head. "Ethan Nance, that is such a 'player' line."

"No, Vanessa, it's the truth." Had he not shown her just how much he cared about her, how no other woman mattered? Maybe she needed clarification. "I'm not interested in anyone but you, and I'm never *going* to be interested in anyone *but* you." He reached out, touched her cheek. "You showed me how good life can be with you. I want that back and if I'm ever fortunate enough to earn another chance, I'm never going to risk losing it again." His voice cracked, but he pushed out the words she needed to hear. "You taught me about real joy and what it means to truly care about someone...to love someone." Pause and one final truth. "I love you in a way I never believed possible, and all I ask is a chance to show you."

A tear slipped down her cheek, followed by a sniff. "Oh, Ethan."

Damn, it was too soon. He should have waited until she grew more comfortable being around him again and—

"I love you, too." Another sniff, a tiny smile.

"You do?" His heart jumped, burst with happiness. "Really?"

A nod, a soft "I was so hurt that you'd kept something so important from me, and I was angry...and empty inside. I didn't know if I could trust you, didn't know if I *wanted* to give you another chance. I thought, why should I? But a person can only live with hurt and anger for so long before it begins to destroy her. The people around me saw that and began to ask the tough questions: can you picture your life without him, or him with someone else, do you want to be with him? And then, do you love him?"

Ethan owed this town a lot and he'd never forget their support or their kindness. He placed his hands on her shoulders, said in a gentle voice, "I'm glad you have such good friends."

"I do, and I've never had that before. They shared their stories and there were some painful ones in there, but they got through it. As I listened to them talk about what happened and how they survived and grew stronger, it gave me hope." She smiled up at him. "And then I kept re-reading the note about hope you sent me and I knew what I wanted to do." Her voice dipped, filled with pure emotion. "I love that note."

If a few heartfelt lines could create that look on her face, well, how could a guy resist? Why would he want to...? "I love you." Ethan framed her face with his hands, leaned toward her. "I've missed you so damn much."

Vanessa traced his lips with her fingers, whispered, "I'm going to kiss you and *then* I'm going to show you just how much I love you. How much I've missed you...and how much I *adore* those notes."

"You are?"

"Oh yes." She brushed her lips over his, once, twice, sighed and deepened the kiss until he was the one sighing. More kissing as she reached for his sweater, eased it along his chest, and over his head. "And then I'm going to take you to bed. But first I want to thank you for not giving up on us."

Ethan removed her sweater, tossed it on the couch, and rested a hand on the waistband of her pants. "I promise I will never keep anything from you again."

"No, you won't." A long kiss, a zipper opening and his pants sliding to the floor. "If you do, you'll be writing a lot of notes."

He ran his tongue along the side of her neck, placed soft

kisses behind her ear. "Do I have to fall out of your grace to write them to you?"

"No, I hope I'll receive them on special occasions...or any occasion." A moan slipped from her lips as he traced the rim of her lace bra, unfastened the clasp.

"I actually have a short one in my head if you'd like to hear it." He'd memorized it last night but recalling the words in his state of 'hot and bothered' could prove a challenge.

"Yes, please."

"Yes, please?" He slid her bra from her shoulders and captured a nipple.

"Oh, Ethan..."

He straightened, tried to focus. "I'll be quick so we can continue getting...*reacquainted*." The look she gave him said she liked that idea, but the kiss that followed told him she had her own ideas on how the getting reacquainted was going to play out. Vanessa did love to be in charge. Ethan cleared his throat, looked into her eyes, and began to speak.

*You walked into my life and changed my world.*
*Filled it with joy and hope and love.*
*Made me believe in possibility.*
*And love.*
*Come walk beside me, hand in hand.*
*As we build our family.*
*Share our love.*
*And become one.*
*Forever.*

The first tear slipped from her cheek to her chin, followed by a second, then a third. "Hey, those better be happy tears."

She swiped her cheeks, nodded. "Only happy tears. That is the most perfect 'I love you' I've ever heard."

Ethan caught one of her tears. "Maybe because you're

perfect." Pause and a hint of a smile. "And that is not a 'player' line."

Her face burst with joy. "I know. That's an I-love-you line." She clasped his hand, turned toward the hallway. "Let's go to bed."

"What about dinner?" He didn't care about anything but feeling her next to him—in bed, naked, lots of pleasure. But it wasn't about him and she was pregnant, and—

"Dinner can wait." She offered him a sultry smile. "I can't." And then she pressed her delicious body against his and captured his mouth in a promise of love, hope, and forever.

# 28

*hree months later*
     Ethan and Vanessa sat in the small living room on a couch they'd purchased in preparation for the baby. Comfort was key, at least that's what the guys told him, and he could see their point. What was the use of filling the house with furniture that belonged in a magazine, but wasn't functional?

Speaking of functional and not something he'd ever imagined getting excited about...gliding rocker chairs. Yup, supposedly they were must-haves so they'd ordered two—one for the nursery and one for the living room. Ethan let out a sigh of pure contentment. Life was great. He and Vanessa sat on their new couch, shoulder to shoulder, eyes closed, breaths even. This had become their form of meditation: the daily gathering, sitting together, eyes closed, sometimes talking, sometimes not. Finding peace. Ethan looked forward to it as a time of real sharing, a word he'd once detested. It was during these times that they talked about dreams and possibilities, opened up in ways that made them stronger, made them learn more about themselves and each other.

"Who would ever believe this would become our form of meditation?" Vanessa sighed, and he felt the smile in her words.

"Definitely not me… or that our cell phones are on silent in the kitchen."

She laughed. "Cell phones on silent in another room. Eyes closed. Minds calm. That *is* a true surprise, but I am so happy we're doing this."

Ethan reached for her hand, traced the wedding band he'd placed there twenty-three days ago. "Me too, Mrs. Nance." After Darcy, he'd never pictured himself in a long-term relationship, much less married. But now he couldn't imagine anything else, could not imagine himself without Vanessa. She gave him purpose. She gave him joy, happiness, love, and a future of possibilities.

"So… You know I don't need a diamond, right? I didn't even need you to formally say the vows, much less write them."

"I know that but you deserve both. The jeweler said the diamond will be ready soon and marrying you?" He squeezed her hand, blew out a calming breath. "That was one of the best decisions I ever made and I didn't even need a spreadsheet or statistics to reach that conclusion. I had all the data I needed." He brought her hand to his lips, kissed her fingers. "I had you. *You*, Vanessa Nance, are my everything."

"I love you, so very much...more than I ever imagined possible." She took his hand, placed it on her belly. "In a few more months our joy will be complete, but I'm not sure we'll be as relaxed as we are right now."

"That's what I hear." Rogan and Luke Donovan loved to tell him about the sleepless nights, the dirty diapers, the spit-up. But they also told him they wouldn't give it up for anything because being a father was the very best job on earth. "Maybe we can create a list or some sort of spreadsheet to help us navigate life with Baby Nance in the house?"

That made Vanessa laugh. "Right, you mean like how to get the baby to stop crying? How to get a full night's sleep?" Another laugh. "Sure, you create that list and let me know what you think. I hear the only way to do this is together but then I hear that's the only way to get through anything...marriage...children...life." Pause and the softest "As long as you're with me, that's all I need."

In his past life, he would have squirmed, cleared his throat, and found a reason to exit the room and the conversation. Truth? There would not have been *any* conversation resembling this one in *any* capacity. Vanessa was different. She was real. She made him want to be better, want to share and grow. "I'm all-in. Are you okay with this house?" It certainly wasn't what either of them were used to, but it was *their* home.

"I love this house, why?"

"Well, at some point we'll have to decide if we're going to stay here or move down the road to a bigger house."

"I guess we'll have to talk about it. Meredith and Daniel asked if we might think about being neighbors."

"Do you like that idea?"

"Maybe in a year or so." Vanessa let out the softest sigh. "I want to create memories right here in our home before we create them somewhere else. Are you okay with that? The small closets, the tiny kitchen...?"

"As long as you're here, I'm okay with all of it."

Another sigh. "Thank you."

"So, speaking of being okay with things, it sounds like your parents are, too." He felt her tense, grow very still.

"So, you talked to them."

He didn't miss the tiny breaths, the questions stuffed in that statement, the anxiety. Ethan moved his hand over her belly in small circles. "Once you gave me the okay, I thought about how to approach them, what the lead-in would be, when I would tell them about the baby." A loud sigh. "It was damn exhausting, so this morning when you were taking a shower, I called them. Your dad's a little uptight—" he laughed, continued to rub her belly "—even for somebody like me, but we got along. I introduced myself as your husband. That was a shocker, but I didn't back down. I told them if they wanted an opportunity to know their grandchild, then they were also going to get to know you, the real you. Vanessa Rodelle Nance, my wife, my best friend. When they realized I wasn't another fortune hunter, they backed down. Your father even told me to call him Conrad. Of course, I shared the many wonderful qualities you possess and wasn't shy about telling them how much I loved you and how I'd do anything to protect you and the baby. I also told them I'd really like them to be part of that equation."

Two sniffs and then a very quiet "What did they say?"

"Your mom asked when they could visit, and your dad said he didn't want to wait until the baby came. I told them that was up to you. They said they tried to contact you several times and you weren't interested, but I let them know you are interested now." He didn't try to hide the emotion in his words when he asked the next question, "*Are* you still interested? It's your choice and I'll support your decision."

There was the shortest hesitation followed by "Yes, I'm interested. They can come. I want them to meet the man who changed my life in the very best way."

Ethan pulled her to him, stroked her back. Kissed her temple. "We can call them later today and set something up." Another kiss, another stroke of her back. "I did venture off the subject a bit and asked about your ex-husband." He buried his face in her hair, breathed the hyacinth-lavender scent. "I think you'll like this part. Your parents were determined your ex would not take advantage of another unsuspecting woman, so they hired someone to follow him and gather information. There was never quite enough to pin an actual crime on him until two years ago. The man is currently serving time for fraud and embezzlement. I don't think he'll be bothering anyone else."

"My parents were involved in that?"

"They were. They got a club of sorts started with investigators all across the country, gathering information and when they'd compiled enough, they turned the information over to the appropriate sources for an arrest and prosecution. I applaud them for coming forward; it shows just how much they care about you."

"I hope it's not just because they were duped or lost money, but it's hard to say."

Ethan pulled her closer, murmured, "We are *not* going down that road, Vanessa. We can't always believe the worst and we're going to give them the benefit of the doubt until they prove otherwise. I heard the remorse in their voices, and I think you'll be happy about the change in them."

"And what of your mother? Is she still planning to move here once the baby comes?"

It was so easy to talk about someone else's parents, but when the subject of his mother came up, that was a little tricky. "That's what she says."

"I think she wants the opportunity to make things right with you and get to know her grandchild *and* her son."

That made him smile. Vanessa had opened his heart, and he was no longer the same person he used to be... "I'm open for whatever she has to offer, as long as you're by my side to help me accept it."

She eased away, traced his lips with her fingers. "Ethan, look at me." He opened his eyes, held her gaze. "I will *always* be here for you, no matter what." She leaned in, kissed him softly on the mouth. "No matter what."

*It's a boy!*

*Proud parents Ethan and Vanessa Nance welcomed a son, Conrad Daniel Nance, on June 10<sup>th</sup> at 6:53 a.m. Mother and baby are fine. Father is exhausted.*

*Thank you for choosing to spend your time reading Pretenders Like Us, and if you enjoyed it, please consider writing a review on the site where you purchased it.*

*If you would like to be notified of my new releases, please sign up at https://www.marycampisi.com*

# ABOUT THE AUTHOR

Mary Campisi is the bestselling author of over 40 emotion-packed, romantic women's fiction novels that center around hope, redemption, and second chances. Set in small towns, these books take readers through the lives of the characters as they encounter, misfortune, disappointment, and challenges to find hope, friendship and, in some cases, love. Growing up in a small town gives Mary a real sense of how people pull together to help others find their true destiny. Her stories will make you laugh *and* cry, but in the end, you'll feel like you want to live in these towns, meet the residents for coffee or share a meal.

Mary's Truth in Lies series, also known as the *A Family Affair* books, takes place in the Catskill Mountains and centers around the discovery of a man's secret family that prompts the question, *Which family is the real one?* The continued success of this series is driven by readers wanting more and she's created an equally compelling one with the Reunion Gap series.

Mary should have known she'd become a writer when at age thirteen she began changing the ending to all of the books she read. It took several years and a number of jobs, including registered nurse, receptionist in a swanky hair salon, accounts payable clerk, and practice manager in an OB/GYN office, for her to rediscover writing. Enter a mouse-less computer, a floppy disk, and a dream large enough to fill a zip drive. The rest of the story lives on in every book she writes.

When she's not working on her craft or following the lives of five adult children, Mary's digging in the dirt with her flowers and herbs, cooking, reading, walking her rescue lab, Henry, or, on the perfect day, riding off into the sunset with her very own hero/husband on his Ultra Limited aka Harley.

If you would like to be notified when Mary has a new release, please sign up at http://www.marycampisi.com/book/book-release-mailing-list/

*To learn more about Mary and her books…*

https://www.marycampisi.com
mary@marycampisi.com

facebook.com/marycampisibooks

twitter.com/MaryCampisi

amazon.com/author/marycampisi

bookbub.com/authors/mary-campisi

Printed in Great Britain
by Amazon

79503374R10140